M000202089

Let Her Go

M. R. Pritchard

SECOND EDITION

>>> → JULY 2022 ← <<<

LET HER GO is a work of fiction. Names, characters, places, and incidents either are the product of the author's imagination or are used fictitiously. Any resemblance to actual persons, living or dead, events, or locales is entirely coincidental.

Copyright © 2022 M. R. Pritchard

All rights reserved. No part of this book may be reproduced or transmitted in any form or by any means whatsoever without express written permission from the author, except in the case of brief quotations embodied in critical articles and reviews. Please refer all pertinent questions to the publisher. All rights reserved. No part of this book may be reproduced or transmitted in any form or by any means, electronic or mechanical, including photocopying, recording, or by an information storage and retrieval system—except by a reviewer who may quote brief passages in a review to be printed in a magazine or newspaper—without permission in writing from the publisher.

ISBN Hardcover: 978-1-957709-09-3
ISBN: Paperback: 978-1-957709-10-9

Second Edition 2022

Printed and bound in the U.S.A

Library of Congress Control Number: 2015908144

Dedication

For those I love.

Let Her Go

M. R. PRITCHARD

April 13, 2010

I have been married to the most attractive man in New Paltz for approximately three months. His name is Alex Sullivan, the owner of Sullivan's Gym. He is charismatic, handsome, and loved by everyone—including my mother. I think she loves him more than she loves me. It's easy to see it in her eyes when she looks at him. They get a little squishy and crinkly in the corners. That's how you should look at someone you love. When she looks at me, the squish and crinkles are gone.

Alex Sullivan is the type of guy she would have expected Tori to marry, not me. Tori is my sister; she is my twin, and we were born a full twenty-four hours apart. She was the expected one, the planned one. Not me. My mom was a bit granola, and by that I mean she didn't go to the doctor much or get her prenatal sonograms done. It was trendy at the time.

So when she went into labor again, after already delivering my perfect sister, everyone was surprised.

I wish I could have been a fly on that wall to see their expressions when I came out. The way I envision the scene is similar to when you get home and open a fast-food bag, only to find your order is screwed up. I bet they took a glance and thought, *We ordered a grilled chicken on a lightly toasted bun with no mayo and lettuce, so slender and healthy. Now where did this greasy double cheeseburger come from?*

It didn't help that I wasn't a pretty baby like Tori. Nope. I was tiny and shriveled, with dark hair and ghostly pale skin. They kept me an extra week in the hospital simply because I looked sickly. It was the only time in my life that I was considered small.

My mom always said she loved us both the same, but it was easy to see she had a favorite: Tori. There were more pictures of her, she got more hugs, she got the fancy, girly-girl bedroom, and she got more presents. She was the baby they planned and prepared for. I got all of the leftovers, even in the gene pool. I'm not sure which parent to thank for the pale skin, the mousy brown hair, and the chubby hips. I'm blaming my dad.

Through it all, I was aware that I wasn't the good-looking sister. Tori was tall, blonde, athletic—just like our mother. And even though we went to the same high school, I rarely saw her. While she was a cheerleader, I was best friends with the librarian. We couldn't have been more different. Most people didn't even know we were related, let alone twins. We were more acquaintances, living in the same house, with the same parents. That's the best way to describe our relationship. She wasn't ruined by our parents' doting, but she never pointed it out to them, and we weren't close enough to talk about how it affected me. That's why I wasn't in the car with her on prom night. I didn't go to prom, I never got asked. Tori did though, by five guys. The guy she finally chose, I don't remember who he was—I hid in my room when he showed up for pictures.

With prom came parties, and with parties came alcohol, and with alcohol came the car accident. Tori died and my parents were left with the daughter they never expected, wanted, and barely loved. They didn't even attend my high school and college graduation ceremonies; they were in Key West.

It was hard to find friends who didn't know about the tragedy of my sister's car accident, so I spent most of my free time alone. It was easier that way. Fewer questions. Plus, with my job as an ER nurse, I got plenty of social time talking with patients and coworkers.

When I met Alex, I had been fresh out of nursing school and just finished my six months of orientation. I have no idea how I landed him. After the long hours at the hospital, night shifts, and crappy food, I added an extra ten pounds had been added to my frame. And being on the tall side of short, ten pounds on me looked like twenty. So what's a girl to do? Sign up at a gym. Sullivan's Gym. The place was one town over and filled with strangers. Easy to avoid conversation or running into anyone who knew me.

It took me a few weeks to figure out that Alex was being more than friendly. I was so used to being the unwanted one and the invisible one that I wasn't used to the attention. I soaked it up, lost the ten pounds, and then I finally accepted his invitation on a date, which turned into a few dates. When he proposed after just a couple of weeks, I didn't think twice before I said yes. I was well aware that I would never catch a guy like Alex again.

We got married at the justice of the peace and bought a little house in New Paltz, far enough to get away but not far from where we both worked. When we moved everything into the house, Alex leaned back on the couch, spread his arms wide, took in a deep breath, and said, "Nice and normal, just like I've always wanted. The American dream."

Well, who doesn't want just a little more than the American dream? Alex was my lotto win. And I was happy with that, even if I had a hard time feeling like I deserved him.

~

"You ready?"

I snap out of it and focus on the man in front of me. Alex is wearing a dark gray V-neck T-shirt and faded jeans.

Turning to the mirror, I take one last look at myself. I'm wearing jeans too and a black dressy top that I spent way too much money on. My eyes zero in on the bulge across my middle. "Does this look okay?"

"Perfect," Alex says.

"I don't really believe you." I spin to check him out again. "What about this area?" I circle my hands around my middle. "This area right here?"

4

He places his hands on his hips and shakes his head. "I don't see it."

"I do. Every time I look in the mirror." I frown at my reflection. "You're all fit and lean and I'm . . . not."

"You're perfect." Alex kisses my cheek. "Come on." He pulls on a jacket. "We're going to be late."

I give up on the mirror.

"Where are we going?" I ask as I pull my own jacket on.

"It's a surprise. Let's get moving." He grabs his keys off the dresser, and we head out the door.

Alex drives toward Poughkeepsie.

"Are we going to your gym?" I ask.

"Not mine." He flashes me his classic smile. It's symmetric, wide, and shows his perfect teeth. It belongs on a supermodel, not the husband who settled for me.

Alex pulls up to a packed parking lot. I miss the sign on the gym; I'm too busy looking at the homemade sign out front. "MMA Heavyweight Fight: Nick Stacks vs. Eddie Vale."

"You brought me to a fight?" I ask.

"Nick's fighting." Alex parks the car. "Gotta support my gym mascot."

Nick is Alex's best friend. I've met him a few times. And by *met* I mean he stood on the other side of the room, never making eye contact with anyone, and I just assumed it was him by Alex's descriptions.

"You've never brought me to a fight before," I say, watching the people file in the front door.

"Well." He unbuckles his seatbelt and reaches for the door handle. "I thought it would be fun, you know, having you there with me for once."

"Okay."

After Alex gets out, I wait for him to open my door. He's always insisted that I wait. A few times I opened the passenger door myself, and he got mad. Well, maybe not mad, but frustrated, like when a person doesn't say much, but you can tell they feel like they let you down. I explained to Alex that I wasn't used to people doing things like that for me. He had looked at me like I was crazy and then explained that every man should treat his wife like royalty, like in the olden days. I let him do it because Alex makes me feel like a queen, and it is addictive.

The energy in the parking lot is electric. Alex takes my hand and we follow everyone inside. We have front-row seats. Alex drops his jacket onto a chair and jumps up into the ring. Nick's there, wearing a pair of glossy black shorts and nothing else. They talk as I take a look around. The place is filled with fancy people: hot chicks in barely there dresses and long blonde hair, dudes with their hair greased back, and a few people I recognize from the gym.

I feel uncomfortably out of place here.

I sit, pull out my smartphone, and load up my e-reader. I started a book last night that's way more interesting than this. I'd rather stare at my phone than at all the other people. I'm two chapters in before the lights in the audience dim.

Alex pats Nick hard on the shoulder before jumping down from the ring and returning to my side.

He kisses me on the cheek as I slide my phone into my pocket.

"Excited?" Alex asks, his eyes wide and twinkling with anticipation.

"Sure." I try not to let my voice sound hesitant, but I think it does.

The lights focus on the ring and the fight starts. I've never seen anything like it. Muscular men, glistening with sweat, moving faster than I've seen anyone move, punching and kicking. One guy goes down and then Nick is on the ground with him. They're grappling right in front of us, like, four feet away. I can hear their breaths as they suck in and out. They're still, then one moves an arm or a leg, trying to trap the other in some tangled position. Suddenly they are off each other, standing on opposite sides of the ring. The ref is making motions with his arms, saying something I can't hear. The crowd stands and Alex pulls me to my feet as he shouts. The ref gives a hand signal, and Nick moves like a wasp, quick and violent. Something sprays across my arm and I'm not sure if it is sweat or blood from the men in the ring, but the crowd roars with excitement. My heart thunders in my chest; sweat starts dripping across the back of my neck. Feeling sick, I start to move away but knock into the guy next to me. I get an elbow in the ribs, and I'm not sure if he meant to do that or if it was accidental because I got in his space. Alex grabs my hand and pulls me toward him. His lips are moving but I can't hear him over the roar of the crowd. Everything is buzzing in my ears and it feels as though my lungs are going to explode out of my chest. Making my way around Alex, I run out of there.

Alex follows. "Morgan!" I finally hear him but I keep running for the door and the fresh air. "Morgan!" he shouts again.

I stop once I get outside and take a deep breath, pulling off my jacket and trying to breathe after being surrounded by all of that. I face him, panting and sweating like a captured animal.

"What's wrong?" Alex asks.

"I can't watch that." My voice sounds panicked.

"It's just a fight."

"No. That . . ." I step away from him and after I rub my face, I jerk a hand toward the event. "That was *brutal*. I can't watch that, Alex."

"Come on, Morg." He smiles and holds his arms out to me. Normally I would just fall into them and take whatever he wanted to give, but right now, I can't. "It's just a fight."

"Just a fight?" The words come out with exasperation. "Just a fight?" I repeat.

"Yeah," Alex responds with a chuckle, like I'm crazy or something.

"I spend my life fixing up people in the emergency room. I mean, just yesterday we had a woman show up who was beat to shit by her boyfriend. It's never just a fight. I can't . . . I just can't watch that." That's when the tears start flowing. I don't want to upset him, but I want to support him and the things he likes to do. And while my eyes are searching his, there is that tiny voice in the back of my mind still asking me why the hell he settled for me.

"Aw, Morg," Alex says as he walks toward me; I don't back away this time. He stops my hands as I try to wipe the tears off of my face. I don't want to cry in front of him. I feel like it does nothing but make me weak and ugly. But I can't control myself. As the tears flow, Alex pulls me into his arms and smooths my hair with his hand. "I'm sorry. I'm sorry." He squeezes me. "I didn't know it would upset you."

I try to get myself together. "Me either. I don't know why. I guess it was just a shock I wasn't prepared for."

Alex leads me away from the building, still holding me tightly under his arm, pressed to his side. "I'll bring you home."

I nod. I'm pretty sure I just ruined our night out. There's no saving it.

"I'm sorry," I say as I sniff and pat my face with my sleeve.

"It's no problem," Alex replies. He doesn't even sound mad or upset. He never does. That's Alex—understanding and considerate. It makes me feel even more like a jerk for ruining the night.

Alex drives me home, handing me tissues from the center console as I try to get my emotions under control. He chews on butterscotch candies as he drives. "Want one?" He holds his hand out and I shake my head no. He always offers them to me when we're in the car, but I can't stand the taste of butterscotch. Once my mother made ten batches of butterscotch oatmeal cookies for a road trip, and whenever we said we were hungry, she'd give us cookies to eat. I haven't been able to stomach the taste since.

When we get inside our house I notice he doesn't take off his shoes or his jacket.

"You're going back?" I ask.

"I have to," he says. "I have to be there for Nick. This is important, and it gets new members to the gym when they see us there together."

I nod, understanding. Alex goes to every fight, and usually I'm at work for them. It's what keeps his gym successful, he tells me. Watching his best friend get beat up then turn around and win—that keeps the customers coming to him for training advice.

Alex kisses me good-bye, and as I hear him start the car and leave the driveway, I head to the freezer and pull out my secret stash of chocolate–peanut butter ice cream. After looking at my bulging midsection in the mirror earlier, my guilty conscience is screaming at me not to eat the entire contents. So I eat half of it, then wrap myself in a throw blanket and open the book I was reading on my phone earlier.

Sitting on the couch alone, I wonder to myself if Alex will cozy up to one of those women at the fight. They watch him like hawks when I'm around, and I bet they're waiting for me to be gone to descend on him. He has never struck me as unfaithful, but there's a lot about my husband that I don't know. I mean, I married him after only knowing him a few weeks. I've never met his family or his friends—other than Nick—and when I ask about them, he always manages to change the subject. Or sometimes he kisses me and tells me I'm everything he needs, and that does nothing but turn me into putty in his hands.

September 26, 2010

"You're drinking," Alex says before he closes the front door.

Refusing to make eye contact and finishing my sip of cold beer, I answer, "Yup."

Alex wants a baby. It's part of his American dream. I tell him we've got more than enough time, but he's been pressuring me little by little with a comment here, a comment there, a magazine article, or pointing out a baby carriage in the mall. It's a bit frustrating since I know being pregnant will only make me fatter. I'm afraid he'll leave me if I get fatter. I'm afraid he'll leave me if I don't get pregnant. The thought of it all scares me. Alex reminds me that even though I think my parents don't love me, I have the opportunity to show my own child how much I love and want them. It doesn't sound so bad sometimes, watching a child bloom under your love. So I agree to a baby and find that making a baby means that I get to see Alex naked a lot more of the time. He's nice to look at naked.

"Thought you were . . . *late.*"

I finally look at him. Alex gives me that look, the one that tells me he's not sure what to say, but he's also afraid to say nothing at all.

"Was." I take a long swallow and relish the sweet burn in the back of my throat.

"When?" he asks.

"Four days ago."

Alex drops his gym bag on the floor. He's disappointed; I can hear it in his movements.

"You didn't tell me," he says.

I frown at my beer, refusing to meet his eyes. "Couldn't. I had to work all those days in a row. I couldn't afford to go *nutso* in the middle of that. People depend on me."

I sniff and swallow down the strange feeling in my throat. Working in the emergency department means people rely on me. They don't give much of a crap if we've been trying to have a baby for months.

"Maybe you should find another job?" I hear him moving around near the door, hanging up his jacket, kicking off his shoes.

"I like my job."

I chose the one career where I am wanted, I am needed, and I am expected. Everyone anticipates a chipper nurse, a nurse made plump by endless snacks and sodas and coffees consumed to help you stay awake all night. Yeah, this career is where I am finally wanted. I am wanted to bandage, console, treat, and teach.

Alex finally moves to stand in front of me. "Every day you're surrounded by it. Don't you think it would be easier if you worked somewhere else? The local nursing home is hiring. Or . . ."

"Or what?" I ask. I want to yell at him. We've had this same conversation so many times. But I don't yell at him. Alex and I just don't do that sort of thing. He's never raised his voice to me, and I've never even thought about it because I'm afraid that's just one more tick mark on the checklist of reasons why I don't deserve him.

"You could quit," Alex offers. "Just stay home or help me at the gym."

I sink deeper into the overstuffed couch. Every single one of my friends at work, within child-bearing age, is either pregnant or has had a baby within the last year. Still, that doesn't mean I want to listen to my coworkers talk about who is pregnant and who will be next. Maybe I've been cursed, drawn to the one occupation that drains me deep down. For a split second, I wonder if my sister were still alive if she would be having this same problem. We were twins, after all. But so far from identical that people didn't even realize we were related when they heard our last names. My mom is right; I would expect Alex to be with her. Not me. Not the short, chubby, brown-haired sister who's so plain, people don't even notice me.

Alex noticed me.

Weird.

"Come on." Alex holds out a hand.

I take another long swallow of the beer. He's always been comforting, and that's why I can't look at him right know. He's like the shirtless wonder on the front cover of a romance novel. I want him. I always do. And I know he'll make me feel good—no, great. But maybe if I hold on to this hurt just a little bit longer, maybe if I let it stew in my chest, maybe it won't hurt as badly next time this happens. I wish he hadn't pushed me so hard to jump on this baby train; it's messing with my head. We're good together. A baby would just add stress—stress that would probably set Alex's brain straight and he'd wonder what the hell he's doing with me and finally move on to one of the nice, young gym girls.

My eyes finally flick up to meet his dark brown ones. The green flecks in them stand out today, making him look even more handsome. The cut-up Sullivan's Gym shirt he's wearing looks too small on him, our last name stretching across the front of it. God, he must've worked out before he locked up. His muscles are tense. His dark hair matted to the back of his neck.

"Want to go out to dinner?" he asks.

"Not really. I just got this book." I hold up the book and look away from his face and stare at the words on the page. What the hell was I reading about anyways? Looking at him seemed to wipe my mind just now.

"Want to rent a movie?" He stands expectantly before me.

"Um . . ." My throat turns thick with want—no, need—no, pure lust. Sitting on the couch with him that close, I find him hard to resist. I could try though, if he sits over on the love seat.

"Sure." I take another sip of the beer. "You want to shower first?"

The corner of his mouth tips up. "Thought chicks liked a sweaty man?"

I swallow hard and watch as he turns and makes his way to the stairs. Then I chug the rest of the beer and listen for the shower to start and wonder why in the hell, out of all the hot bodies he had strutting all over that gym he runs, why he chose me? I only went there for a few weeks and haven't been back.

"Men like me, we like curves." That's what he told me last time I asked him. Well, that's a good thing, because I've got plenty of those.

I stare at the pages of my book, talking myself out of going upstairs and getting a look at him in the shower. I really want to look at him in the shower. He's nice to look at. By the time I work up the nerve and uncurl my legs from underneath me, it's too late. Alex walks down the stairs, his hair still damp, shirtless, and a pair of loose sweatpants sitting low across his trim waist. He turns the TV on, grabs the remote, and sits down next to me. I peer over the edge of my book. He smells fresh from the soap and shampoo and deodorant. God, a million women would kill to be me right now, sitting next to this ripe specimen of a man with his six-pack abs and toned body. I raise the beer to my lips only to be met with a trickle. Damn, I forgot I drank it all already. I move to get up.

"Where are you going?" he asks as he presses the buttons on the remote and starts flicking through the movie rental channel.

"Beer. Want one?"

"Sure." His eyebrows pull together as he focuses on his task.

Just as I make it to the fridge, my cell phone rings.

I stand in the entrance to the kitchen, watching Alex as I listen to the charge nurse begging me to come in because they're shorthanded and everyone in town has come down with the flu this week.

Alex turns and frowns. He knows what I'm about to do. He shakes his head from side to side in a pleading *no*, a begging *no*, a stay-home-with-me *no*.

I think about the beer I just drank. It was one beer; by the time I'm ready for work it will have worn off.

I say yes and hang up the phone.

"Morgan!" Alex says, disappointment evident in his deep voice.

"They need help and it's double time." I think of the recent addition to the gym: the four saunas he just had installed. I could pay them all off with this one twelve-hour shift. Not that he's ever complained about the money, but I like to do my part to help out.

"You just did five days in a row," he argues.

"I know, but we can pay off the saunas with the money from this."

"I don't care about the money. I want to spend time with you. You've been working all week."

I know what will happen if I stay. We'll each drink a few more beers, and then the movie won't matter; we'll be stripping each other naked and rolling in bed before it's even over.

"Tomorrow," I promise, bending to kiss his cheek as I pass him to run up the stairs and change for work.

Just before running out the door, I stop near the couch and straddle him.

"I love you, lover," I say as I press my lips hard to his and instantly wonder why the hell I'm going back there tonight.

Alex wraps his arms around me, squeezing me to his firm chest like he doesn't want to let me go. "It's not too late to cancel." His hands slide down to my waist and pull my hips tight against his.

Oh Jesus. A little tingle springs up my back.

"Last shift. Then I'm yours for almost two weeks. No work after this, I promise," I say.

"You better." He slaps a hand on my backside and slips his tongue in my mouth. He tastes like beer and he's so warm. His skin is soft and smooth.

Why the hell am I leaving him here like this?

I pull away and stand up to adjust my uniform, resisting the temptation to give in.

"I'll beep in the morning when we drive by each other," I say. We'll see each other on my way home in the morning since we drive down the same road, each headed in different directions.

"Okay." Alex turns the TV off just as I close the door.

September 27, 2010

The air is thick with a cold fog as I leave work the next morning. The sunrise is a foreboding blue-gray. It's such a strange combination that I stand next to my car and take it all in.

I should have known something bad was going to happen.

My phone dings with a text message from Alex.

Taking the bike. Please don't hit my truck in the driveway.

I look up at the overcast morning sky and wonder why he would be riding his motorcycle to work when it looks like it might rain.

K. Love you, I text back.

Remember, no work. You're mine for 2 weeks. See you when I get home.

Will beep. I add a little heart emoticon when I send the message. I open the driver's side door to my little car, throw my work bag onto the passenger seat, start the engine, and pull out of the parking lot.

There are twelve deer standing on the side of the road, seeming to watch me as I drive. I drop my speed to a crawl. The last deer bows its head. I smile to myself, thinking the buck is nodding a good morning to me.

It's a thirty-minute commute and as I pass the second turn on the weaving road, I search the other lane, waiting to get a glimpse of Alex's red motorcycle. I'll beep and wave and he'll just tip his head, like he always does. It's fine. I prefer he keeps both of his hands on the handlebars.

When I get to the next curve in the road, I notice bright lights flashing and slow to a stop. There's a trooper in front of me holding out his hand. There are flares in the road, broken glass, and way too many undamaged Crown Victorias. I lean to the side looking for the accident, but instead of a car I see a trail of blood, smeared thick across the two-lane road. Near the edge there is a black hoof and the fawn-brown coloring of a deer. It's lying lifeless near the shoulder, head tilted at an odd angle, its full rack of antlers smeared with blood.

The trooper in front of me walks closer. Assuming he's seen my scrubs and the stethoscope around my neck, I put the car in park and reach for the door. By the time I'm standing, the trooper's walking toward me faster with both hands out, his mouth open, ready to say something. But now that I'm standing, I see the vehicle, except it's not a car. It's a motorcycle. A red motorcycle.

My heart starts beating hard. Really hard. Harder than during my first code in the emergency room.

Alex!

I'm not sure how I make it past the line of troopers. All I know is I make it to him and fall to my knees, feeling the burn of the pavement through my thin scrub pants. There are sirens blaring behind me.

"Oh my God, Alex!" I hear my voice shouting. He looks pale, so pale, and his mouth is rimmed blue. "What happened? Why is no one doing anything?"

My real life clicks off as my nursing training clicks on. I reach for him, feeling his neck, just like they drilled into my brain for years. There's nothing. I struggle to move his shoulders. I tip his head, and placing my lips on his, I give him two breaths.

"I need help with this," I shout to the officers.

As I move my hands over his chest, I don't need to count ribs or measure. I know every inch of Alex's perfect body and exactly where to give compressions. Positioning the heels of my hands, I start counting under my breath, running the tune "Staying Alive" through my head to keep a steady beat.

The sirens stop. There are boots running, voices talking. When I get to one hundred, I press my lips to his and give two more quick breaths. I move to resume compressions.

Why the hell aren't the EMTs helping? I only have a split second to wonder; I'm too busy counting.

Someone kneels across from me. All I see is a blue uniform—not a face, or a gender, or anything—just blue. In this moment, I hate the color blue. It's the same shade as Alex's lips.

"Two breaths," I tell them. "Then I need you to take over compressions."

An arm reaches out, not touching me but tipping up my hospital ID tag.

"Morgan?" a voice asks.

"Yeah." I stop my counting for just a second. "I'm going to do breaths. I need you to do chest compressions."

"Morgan." The voice sounds strange.

"Help me!" I'm almost out of breath; my arms ache from trying to pump the life back into him. "Help me!"

"How many sets have you done?"

"I don't know. He needs a breath. Help me!" I'm yelling at the person. I move, pressing my lips to Alex's again. The blue uniform doesn't move but only leans away.

"What the hell?" I continue. "If you're not going to help me, get someone that will!"

"Morgan."

"What do you want?" I shout at the uniform.

"It's too late."

"Wha . . . No, no! I just got here. It's not too late. I just need help." I pause. *Damn!* Now I've lost count. I give him two more breaths then move to give more compressions.

Suddenly, I sense someone behind me, another at my side, and the uniform in front of me, all giving me an intense look.

"Let's go! Get the AED. Get something. What the hell are you people doing?" I shout, pressing my palms to Alex. My arms are burning and I don't know how much longer I can continue doing this alone.

The blue uniform grasps me by my shoulders. "Morgan!" They shake me a little. "He's gone. They did CPR for twenty minutes before you showed up."

"What? No. No one was doing anything. Why isn't anyone doing anything?" I yell at them, shrugging the hands off of my shoulders and my arms. I continue to pump his chest.

"He's gone, Morgan."

"No!" I shout.

"Yes." The voice is soft. "He's gone."

"NO!" I scream.

"Look at his leg," the voice pleads.

My eyes move; my arms stop. His jeans are ripped and I see a large gash across his upper thigh. There's so much blood. At first I thought it was from the deer, but it's pooled under his legs, near the wound on the inside of his thigh. Something clicks in my brain.

"Femoral artery."

"Yes. Morgan. The antler sliced it clean through. They already did CPR. They already tried to resuscitate. He bled out."

My eyes move to the blue uniform in front of me. I finally see her face—an older woman with brown curly hair and big brown eyes. "Morgan. I am *so* sorry. You weren't meant to see this. They were just waiting for the doctor to call back and confirm time of death."

My heart stops.

"No." My lips tremble and my eyes burn.

"Yes." She nods her head.

I focus behind her and notice bystanders on the far side of the blockade. One raises his cell phone and takes a picture. Others have their phones raised. *They're filming the entire thing. I bet it looks amazing with the hazy blue sky—real foreboding and dreary.*

"But . . . but . . . I heard sirens. There were sirens."

She gives a long blink and shakes her head. "I'm sorry. Not for him."

"Who?"

She tips her head and gives me a knowing look. It's for me, in case I faint or freak out or try to resuscitate my dead husband in the middle of the road.

"You want us to call someone for you?" she asks.

I feel my mouth hang open for a minute as the numbness settles throughout my body and something deflates in my chest. My fingertips tingle. My brain searches for words. "My parents are out of town. On a cruise. Alaska."

"Anyone else?"

I shake my head no. I only have Alex. I only had Alex.

The people around me move, draping a piece of fabric over his body and guiding me away, toward the open back door of an ambulance. As I sit in the back of the ambulance, staring at the sheet covering my husband's body in the road, I hear a familiar voice. It's Nick Stacks, Alex's best friend. He must've heard or went investigating when Nick didn't show up at the gym. I never even thought to call him.

The lady in the blue uniform walks him over to me.

Nick nods, not saying my name or doing much to acknowledge me—not that he ever did.

"I'll give her a ride home," Nick tells the lady.

I don't think I've ever heard him speak before.

For a second I want to tell him no, but I stop myself, realizing that a twenty-minute drive with Nick will be quiet. He may have been Alex's best friend,

23

but he never wanted anything to do with me, it always seemed. I just assumed he didn't like me. He's never spoken to me, never said two words, and has always given me the cold shoulder. I never liked him much either, but right now, with the past hour so fresh in my mind and the loss so strong in my heart, there's no better person I can think of to take me home.

I follow Nick to his truck and let myself in through the passenger door. It feels strange, opening the passenger side door myself after having Alex do it for me all this time. Nick says nothing. I say nothing. Since he knows where I live, I don't have to give him directions.

Nick pulls up in front of my house.

"I'll have one of the guys get your car home," he says, his first words to me since I met him almost six months ago.

With a small nod, I get out, walk inside, and stand there, alone and numb.

There is thunder, then lightning, and the sky erupts into a torrential downpour. I've heard people say that rain is good luck on your wedding day, and such; it washes everything away so you can start anew. I don't want it to wash Alex away. Nothing sounds more terrible to me right now than washing everything I had with Alex away and starting over from scratch. He was the only one who ever wanted me.

I drop down onto the couch, and as I'm lying there, wrapped in the throw blanket that smells like Alex and staring at our picture on the wall, I wonder what the morning sky looked like the day my sister died. I can't remember. I don't even remember what Tori looked like in her prom dress before she died. I can't remember much right now. All I know is that I just lost the best thing that ever happened to me. The one person who noticed me. The one person who didn't look past me. Who made me feel like I wasn't the unwanted one for once. I am so afraid of forgetting anything about him.

September 30, 2010

Every nurse's nightmare is to have a family member as a patient. What happened to me took that fear to another level. There's nothing worse than the events of three days ago. I am pretty certain of that.

I make the mistake of turning on the television. I should have never turned on the television because now I'm staring at myself on the screen, on my knees, frozen in shock over Alex's body. We made the evening news, my dead husband and I. Flashes of images of me trying to resuscitate him, giving breaths, looking at the wound on his leg, the blood smeared across the road, the dead deer. Then there is the person in the blue uniform. I heard her voice, felt her hands on my shoulders, but the entire time, I was looking at Alex's body trying to convince myself that this wasn't real. I forgot what she looks like. She can't be much older than me.

The last image on the television screen is of me sitting in the back of the ambulance, scowling at the crowd, with mascara streaking down my face. The press has had a field day with that picture. Then Nick shows up on the television screen. That's when the party stops. The news stream ends just as he parks his huge body right in front of me, blocking them from filming or taking any more pictures. I wonder for a split second if he did that on purpose. No, he didn't—he couldn't. Nick doesn't care about anyone else but himself. Must've been pure coincidence.

With Nick's simple movement, suddenly all of my parents' actions make sense from when Tori died in that car accident back in high school. They wouldn't let me watch TV or go online or read the papers. After her funeral, they whisked me away on a vacation to Europe for three weeks. "We just need to get away," my mother had said. Now I see why.

Everyone loves a tragedy.

Everyone exploits a tragedy.

I wonder if maybe I should go away right now. Maybe I should pack my suitcase and take off for someplace tropical and warm. No. I wouldn't do that. That's what my mother does; she runs away from everything that might cause her pain. She ran from Tori's death, and does so on each anniversary. When I finally get them on the phone to tell them what happened to Alex, I know she's going to do the same thing.

My mouth dries and I look down at Alex's half-folded T-shirt in my hands. I press it to my face and breathe in deep. What I wouldn't give for one more second with him sitting by my side on this couch. I should have stayed home and watched a movie with him that night.

The doorbell rings. It's dinged every day at least once. I've never opened it, though. I couldn't face anyone and I saw the news truck parked in the street for the past two days. Glancing out the window, I see it's finally gone.

Maybe it's time to open the door.

I make my way to the front door and open it. There stands hulking Nick, muscles bulging in a black shirt, looking horribly enormous next to Mr. Peterson. Why is the mayor at my house? And why is my dead husband's best friend at my house? He couldn't even show up to our wedding. Why would he bother showing up now?

"Morgan." Mr. Peterson moves toward me. "Can we come in?" he asks.

I step away from the door and let them in. I don't bother to sit down; I just stand in the middle of the living room with my arms crossed.

"The neighbors have been calling me," Mr. Peterson says as he takes a quick glance around the room. "I know this has been terrible, just terrible." He moves around the living room, glancing at the pictures on the wall and the stack of laundry near the couch. "But I just wanted to stop by and, on behalf of the residents of New Paltz, deliver our sincerest apologies for your loss."

"Thank you." It comes out as a croak and I realize I haven't spoken to another person since Nick dropped me off at my house. Even then I didn't speak to him. I only spoke to the woman in the blue uniform and asked her why the hell she wasn't helping me. Actually, I think I screamed at her.

Nick starts moving in and out of the house. It takes me a moment watching him to see that he's carrying in piles of mail, bulging brown grocery bags, and pans of casseroles. When he's done taking everything to the kitchen, he stands awkwardly next to Mr. Peterson.

"Morgan?" Mr. Peterson asks. I get the feeling he's been talking this entire time, but I've been staring off into space and blocking him out. When I focus on him, he says, "You'll let us know if you need anything, won't you?"

I nod.

"Good. Good." I think he hugs me before he leaves. I'm not quite sure, but I think I feel his fingertips trailing a pattern on my forearm as he says, "Take care of yourself. Your neighbors have been worried. They haven't seen much of you over the past few days. Our town takes pride in protecting its own during these times of need. We're here for you."

And then he is gone.

I stare at the open front door. Minutes pass before a dull beeping breaches my thoughts. Recognizing it as the oven, I go to the kitchen to investigate. Nick is there, standing at my stove, setting the oven temperature. I don't remember him moving away from Mr. Peterson's side, but for a few moments there, I'm pretty sure I was off in la-la land.

"What are you doing?" I manage to ask him.

Nick barely glances at me as he slides one of the casserole dishes into the oven.

"When's the last time you ate?" he asks.

I shrug. I don't remember and I don't really care.

He starts emptying the bags and putting things in my fridge and cupboards. There's milk, juice, bread, premade salads, and sandwiches. He looks so out of place in our little house. I mean *my* little house. I'm alone in it now. He crosses his arms and leans against the counter. I don't think Nick and I have ever been in the same room for longer than ten minutes. His eyes flick to mine for just a second, and I notice that they're red rimmed and sunken.

"You want to take some of that food?" I ask.

"No." He shakes his head and stands. "Got a fight tomorrow night. All these carbs will make me sick."

Since I have nothing to say, and it seems he has nothing to say, we stand in silence and watch the oven timer tick.

Nick pulls the dish from the oven, and then a plate from the cupboard, before he scoops out what looks like macaroni and cheese and puts it on the plate. He slides it toward me across the counter.

My stomach churns, but not with hunger. I think I might throw up.

"Oh, almost forgot." Nick reaches into his pocket and pulls out a set of keys. "Brought your car back."

"That was days ago." I wonder how long it's been sitting on the side of the road.

He crosses the kitchen and hangs the keys on the little hook by the door. "Actually, they've been in your mailbox since . . ." He doesn't need to tell me what day it was. I know.

"Oh." So things turn awkward. He did what he said but I assumed he didn't because the only Nick I've ever known is the selfish jerk who's too busy pumping iron and fighting in the Octagon. The Nick I'm familiar with doesn't say one word to me.

"Sorry," I whisper.

Nick crosses the kitchen to turn the oven off. "You should probably eat something. You already look like you've lost a few pounds."

Suddenly I'm self-conscious. I could stand to lose a few pounds, but I have the distinct feeling that he just insinuated that I'm fat. I'm definitely not a gym rat, but I'm not obese, just . . . full. After I look at the plate of food, my stomach churns again. Pissed and sad, I leave the kitchen and return to the couch and the laundry basket full of Alex's clothes. Alex didn't care that I was a little plump. He liked it and told me so.

Men like me, we like women with curves. You're perfect, just like this.

Nick doesn't say good-bye. He just closes the door with a gentle click of the lock.

There goes the one person I've heard from since Alex died. I haven't heard from my parents. Usually they call when they are out of international waters and can make a phone call without it costing them twelve dollars a minute.

At least one good thing has come of this day: now I can form a coherent sentence.

The next mistake I make is opening my laptop. Someone set up a page dedicated to Alex with a donation fund. A goddamned donation fund. A few of the names I recognize from the limited stories of Alex's life. But a donation fund? No one even asked me. No one even called. People as far away as Nevada are currently saying prayers for me and talking about my handsome husband as though they knew him personally. The Facebook sidebar is showing that the goddamned story is *trending*, people are *liking* and *sharing* it all over the place. My story, my life with Alex, is currently the diarrhea of the Internet, spreading like the stomach bug in a preschool. There is a Twitter hashtag: *#foreveryoung*. The picture of me giving chest compressions has thousands of *likes* and *shares*. How strange is that, to *like* the most tragic event of my life. You *like* that? Try living it. It's not very likeable.

This is bullshit. The media has made everyone my best friend, when the truth of it is I've never felt more alone. I slam my laptop closed and throw it on the floor. I control the urge to kick it against the wall; so instead, I shove the thing in a cupboard under the kitchen island. Then I take the battery out of my phone and throw it in the basket where I keep hats and mittens for the winter. Next, I unplug the television and close the doors to the entertainment stand. Then I throw the macaroni and cheese in the garbage.

I don't *like* this.

I hate it.

October 1, 2010

My appetite is gone; I can't even stand the smell of food. I think the things Nick brought in the other day are just going to sit in my fridge and rot since I haven't opened any of it. I can't sleep or read or watch television. Sometimes I just sit on the couch and stare at the wall. Sometimes I lie in bed and press my face into his pillow and just . . . breathe. I wonder how long I can go before I will need to change the sheets again.

The phone rings once and I recognize the cell phone number on the caller ID.

It's my parents.

"Hello," I answer.

"Hi, Morgan!" My mother's excited voice is on the other line. "Alaska has been amazing." There is the buzz of people in the background and my father's voice. "How are you?" she asks.

I don't know any other way to say it than point blank. "Alex died in a motorcycle accident five days ago."

There, I told my parents. That makes it real. He's really dead now. He's #foreverdead, not #foreveryoung.

I decide I hate the Internet as well. And Alaska.

"Oh, no . . ." I hear my mom drop the phone.

Did she drop the phone when the troopers called to tell her about Tori?

"What is it?" My father's voice asks. "Morgan?" I can hear my mother in the background, making noise, saying incomprehensible words. My father picks up the phone. "Morgan, what's happened?"

I tell him the same thing I told her. "Alex is dead." And then I tell him everything else.

There is a long silence. I'm sure they're remembering Tori and everything they went through when I was a teenager.

"Jesus . . ." Dad starts. "We're in Anchorage right now, just got cell service on the cruise. We'll catch the first flight home."

"No, Dad, you don't—"

"Yes. We do. We'll be home by tomorrow, I'm sure. Hang in there, girlie."

"Okay," I mumble into the phone, feeling another onslaught of tears bubbling up inside me.

"We love you. Be home soon."

I'm not sure why our family seems to be cursed by death. First Tori, now Alex. They'll come home for a few days, long enough for a hug from each of them and a home-cooked meal. My mother will be heartbroken over Alex. Then she'll run away to some foreign country to forget it all.

October 8, 2010

After seven days I can't even stand to be in the same room with myself. I have no more tears left to cry. I clean the house, fold all of Alex's laundry, hang his shirts next to mine in the closet, and when there is nothing left to do, I pace the living room and stare out the window into the night.

The house next door goes up for sale and the older couple that lives there moves their things out. It occurs to me again that maybe I should move away from here. I sit and watch, and as the day moves on, I catch my reflection in the windowpane. I look terrible but I don't look away. I need to see myself as I am right now: alone and unwanted, again.

It's a good thing I'm used to the feeling, I tell myself. A lesser person would be too emotional to scrape herself off the floor right now. Not me.

I can handle this.

I think I can handle this.

I can handle this, right?

Eventually the sun dips past the horizon. Ah, darkness, my old friend, my only constant. There is something about working the nightshift that makes you welcome the night. You get to see the world with a new perspective—one that ninety-five percent of the population misses.

When I can't stand the sight of my own shadow one second longer, I slip my sneakers on and run out into the night. I'm not sure what compels me to do it—to leave the house, jump off of the porch, and start running down the street. I run fast and hard, with every last bit of energy left in my body. A part of me is hoping that it might exhaust me so I don't feel anything anymore.

I run down my dimly lit street and catch a few curtains moving in my neighbor's windows. I bet they've been watching my house, waiting for the moment I finally left so they can talk about it over their morning coffee. A sob catches in my throat and threatens to choke me. For half a second I consider letting it, but the lack of oxygen pings me in the head, and I scream it out.

Bet the neighbors love that.

I run until I reach the dark park almost three miles away. It's not a children's park but rather one of those parks with benches and paved walkways and flower boxes. I collapse on the grass, breathing hard, mind numb, body tired. I have never run much farther than down a hall during an emergency or to stop a pot from boiling over on the stove. It is a feeling I have never experienced, an exhilaration followed by an exhaustion like I have never known. My throat burns, my thighs burn, my heart burns. I have reached the point at which my body and soul are at maximum ache.

I thought I could handle this, but maximum ache, it hurts like a bitch.

Hearing a strange noise, I sit up a little bit, as much as my sore body will allow. Wiping my face, I blink a few times and as my vision clears, I think I see a deer walking at the forest edge on the far side of the park.

Normally, I would think nothing of a deer, but this one has antlers, and all I can see is that gash on Alex's leg, clouding my vision. I want someone to blame for his death, so I decide I'm going to blame that deer. Any deer I see, I will hate, just as much as I hate the Internet and #*foreveryoung* and Alaska and fundraisers for handsome dead men.

~

I repeat this evening run for weeks.

Sometimes I eat dinner with my parents and do my best to avoid their piteous glances. This is hard for them too, I tell myself. My mother losing two people she loved more than me. She's going to take a week-long cruise to Bermuda in a few days, because that's what she does when things go wrong. She doesn't stick around and make sure I'm okay; she runs away to sunshine and sandy beaches. Paradise is her mourning stone, but the night is mine and I run until I can't feel anymore. I run until the two pairs of yoga pants I have are so loose I have no choice but to get new ones. I run until nothing in my wardrobe fits me anymore. I run until I have to start replacing things: pants, shirts, underwear, bras. None of it fits any longer. And then I find myself doing strange things like shopping for new running sneakers and sports bras in my free time.

November 5, 2010

I received a phone call from a lawyer yesterday. Not just any lawyer. Mr. Peterson, the oldest mayor in America, who also happens to be the oldest lawyer in America, and the only lawyer in the village of New Paltz.

Mr. Peterson doesn't have a receptionist at his office. And really, his office is nothing but a living room with a large desk and a hundred filing cabinets. He sees me on the other side of his glass front door, and before I can knock, he's waving me inside.

"Thanks for coming down so quickly." Mr. Peterson stands and walks around his desk, relieving the only other chair in the room of a stack of folders and files. "Here, have a seat."

I sit.

"You said you needed to speak to me about something?" I ask. His message actually said he needed to speak to me about something *very important* and to meet with him as soon as possible.

"Yes." Mr. Peterson moves behind his desk again. As he sits, he pulls out a manila envelope and opens it. His fingers seem nimble for his age as he shuffles the papers. "Did you know your husband had a will?"

"No." I shake my head. "He never mentioned it."

"Well." Mr. Peterson clears his throat and plucks a paper out of the stack in front of him. "He left you half of his gym."

"Half?" I look away from the papers. I haven't thought about the gym, not for one second. I never even considered that I needed to do anything with it. I was too busy making funeral arrangements and dealing with the life insurance company, and trying to notify Alex's family of his death. The process ended in a lot of dead ends. Alex had told me his parents died not long after he graduated high school. He didn't tell me how; he just clammed up, and I didn't press him. I figured he'd tell me when he was ready. That's the thing I've learned with being a nurse: people will tell you things as their trust in you grows. I never found any more of his family. I was waiting. And now I'll never know if there were people who loved him too.

"Yes," Mr. Peterson continues, "he left you half. He left the other half to a friend of his. Nick Stacks."

"Nick?"

"You know Nick, right?" Mr. Peterson asks. His brows rise in a hopeful look.

"Well." I shrug a bit. "I know who he is. But I don't know much about him."

There's no good way to say that I didn't get along well with Alex's best friend. Or maybe, I never tried to get along with him because he was always so stoic and standoffish.

"He's already asked to buy you out."

Nick "The Strangler" Stacks wants to buy out my share of my husband's business before the dirt even settles on his grave. The idea irritates me.

"How much did you know about your husband, Morgan?" Mr. Peterson asks. This strikes me as strange.

"Enough," I answer. "He had his business and I had my job at the hospital. I didn't need to know his business particulars. The bills got paid, we had food, and we were comfortable when it came to money." Even though I was always working hard to make more. I don't add that last part. Looking back on it now, I feel a bit guilty about it.

"Well." Mr. Peterson tips his head and reaches for a pen. He makes check marks on the paper and slides it across the desk toward me. "There is money too. A significant amount left in a trust fund. In addition to the insurance money." I reach forward to take the pen in his hand and sign, but Mr. Peterson doesn't let go. "He left it all to you." His eyes pierce me like he's sticking a pin in a defining moment in my life.

"Okay." I exhale a stuttered breath. I don't understand what he's getting at. I just know I want to get the heck out of here.

Mr. Peterson releases the pen and I sign my name on the lines. I don't even look at the paper. I couldn't care less what he left me. He never told me about it, and I don't care about it. All the money in the world can't take away the pain of his death. I'd give it all back to have Alex in my life again.

"I'm very sorry for your loss. Alex was a good man." Mr. Peterson shuffles papers before twisting in his office chair and making copies of everything I've just signed. "So are you going to sell your share to Nick?" he asks.

"No." It comes out too quickly, before I have a chance to think about it. I know nothing about running a business.

"Didn't think you would." Mr. Peterson sits back down in his chair and faces me.

"Why's that?"

"Easy. It's your last connection to Alex. When you're ready, you'll let it go. Just not now."

Peterson taps a stack of papers on his desk, straightening each side before sliding it into a manila envelope. As he passes it across the desk to me, he says, "Reckon you'll be able to quit the ER now."

I shrug. "I don't think I'll quit."

"Take a look at the paperwork, Morgan. You're an important part of our community here in New Paltz, but if you need a new start, you can definitely afford it. I thought about it a few times after my wife died, but now I have people who mean a lot to me here. Stay or go. No one will judge you for either decision."

"Sure." I swallow down the thickness in my throat and blink back the burning behind my eyes. It's been two months. I should be able to hold a conversation about him. But I can't. I focus on the wall behind Mr. Peterson until he tells me good-bye, and I get up to leave.

The autumn wind smells sweet with decaying leaves, and I pull my jacket tight around my body as I head to my car. This was the time of the year that I enjoyed most, hiding in loose sweatshirts and sweaters. Now my favorite jacket is too large on me, and the biting wind chills me to the bone. I miss the warmth those extra pounds gave me.

I sit in my car with the sun warming my skin and my manila envelope filled with the things that Alex hid from me. I open the top and pull out a sheet and gasp. There's a trust fund with more than enough money to keep me going for the rest of my life without my ever needing to work again. I feel a sting of regret. I never needed to work that extra shift to pay off the saunas. Alex had more than enough money to buy them outright. Why didn't he tell me? I could have spent the night with him one last time. And if I were home he would have left late for work that next morning and missed the deer. He probably would have taken his truck because it rained later that morning.

What if.

What if.

What if.

I can't stop thinking about all the *what-ifs*.

Who was Alex? And who was I? I wasn't the trophy wife that a man with that much money usually goes for. I wasn't young and skinny and barely fresh out of college. No. I was a hardworking middle-class American. There was nothing extravagant or fancy about me. I wore no jewelry or trendy clothes. We didn't even drive expensive vehicles. Our lives could have been so different together. We could have lived in a brownstone in the city. I could have stayed home and done whatever it is the housewives in New York City do. I could have driven a Mercedes and had a two-carat diamond ring. I could have done all the things that those women do to make themselves look thinner and prettier. I could have bought my mother's love and buried my sister's memory.

There are so many *could-haves*. But when I think hard about it, all of those things are not me. I think I would have been pretty miserable living that life. Maybe Alex had something going with his American dream.

November 15, 2010

"You don't have to come back full-time." Cynthia looks over her glasses at me. She's the nurse manager of the emergency room. "It's okay, Morgan. Really."

"I'm fine," I say.

I'm fine.

I think I'm fine.

I'm fine, right?

"You're not fine," Cynthia says.

The manager before her fired one of our nurses for taking extra time off after the death of a family member. I don't think Cynthia would fire me. She still has her soul—something the medical field seems to suck out of people at an alarming rate. Still, I can't lose my job. It's the only stability I have right now. Without the distraction of work, I'm not sure where my head would be.

"It's in the wrong place," Cynthia says like she just read my mind.

"What?" I ask.

She taps her temple. "Your head's in the wrong place. Should be on healing, spending time with family. Remembering the good times. You should be taking this time for yourself."

"No." I close my eyes and focus. "I'm fine. I need to be back at work."

Cynthia takes off her glasses and lets out a breath of frustration. She glances away for a split second before focusing back on me, making me shift uncomfortably in my seat. "This time is not for work. The Lord did not make us invincible; he did not ask Noah to build an ark because he thought we could survive the great floods. He knew we wouldn't survive. Noah's ark brought his family closer together, taught them to support one another. Every living person has an "Ark"—your family and your support system that keeps you emotionally stable. Your Ark holds you up when you are weak and prevents you from turning to mush and rotting from the inside out. Those people without an Ark, who live through what you've lived through, they simmer in bitter hatred for all the joys in life."

Wow. I blink at her.

"Don't look at me like that, Morgan. Just because I believe in God doesn't mean I'm some wack job. I've seen girls like you in here before. Hell, I can smell you from across the street. You call your job your home; your coworkers, your family; your patients, your social hour. That's not how it works." She pauses, but I have nothing in response. "You know what this job is like. Your head needs to be in the right place when a train wreck walks through those doors." She motions to the ER behind her office door. "You are their lifeline. Now tell me who is yours? Who is your *Ark*?"

She sits there in front of me and waits. I search my brain. It *was* Alex. And now it's . . . no one.

"I don't have anyone right now," I tell her.

Cynthia puts her glasses back on and looks at some papers on her desk. "Where are your parents?"

Thinking back to the last message my mom left on my phone, I reply, "India."

She looks at me, a bit confused.

"They travel a lot. Look, can I just have my schedule?" I ask.

With a huff, Cynthia pulls a sheet of paper out and hands it to me. When I grasp it in my fingers, she doesn't let go. "This is your first warning," she whispers. "You'll crumble from the inside out."

I pull the sheet from her fingers. "I've made it this far being Arkless," I say as I stand. "I'll survive."

"Surviving isn't living," she snaps at me. "You'll only receive so many warnings before you can't turn back."

As I make my way to my car, I glance at my schedule. It's all over the place: one day on, one day off, followed by three days on and two days off. They must've plugged me into openings. Or Cynthia is using this schedule as leverage to get me to take more time off. It's fine, though, I'll just fill in all the days off with extra shifts. I'll prove to Cynthia she's wrong.

I open my car door and get in, noticing the manila envelope resting on the passenger seat. I should really bring it inside and file it away. But it seems I can barely stand to look at the envelope knowing it's filled with the most significant lie my handsome husband never told me. I wonder what else he decided not to tell me? I set my schedule on top of it and head for home, taking the same route I've always taken.

There's a dusting of snow on the side of the road. I don't think much about it until I come to the spot where Alex died and see a white cross sticking out of the ground where they found his motorcycle. The streaks of blood have finally been washed away by weeks of rain.

I pull over and get out. Zipping my coat to my chin to ward off the chill, I wait until there's a break in traffic so I can cross the street. My boots make a hollow sound on the frozen pavement as I approach the shrine. Resting on the ground are pixilated images of him in clear frames, silk flowers, and poems. I left none of this. What kind of wife am I? A few names signed to notes and pictures I recognize from that one time I looked at his Facebook page.

"Hey!" a man's voice shouts from behind me. I turn, only to find myself looking into the lens of a camera. A flash goes off and I shield my face. "You're his wife, right?" the man asks.

Before I can answer, he takes another picture. I back up, blinking away the spots in my vision. I barely get a look at the guy's face before he snaps another picture; the camera never leaves his hands. As I close my eyes to protect them from the bright flash, a car horn beeps, and I feel the air move as it passes way too close to me.

"Hey, don't step in the road," the man says, still moving closer to me. "That would be a tragedy, right? Both of you dying in the same spot."

What a jerk.

Before I can say anything, a strange, deep-toned grunt rips through the air. Moving my hands away from my face, I find a large deer has stepped out of the cover of the mostly bare trees. It has a full rack of horns; eight points I count before the creature takes a step toward the man with the camera. The deer makes the sound again, tipping its head at the man.

"Whoa. Whoa, buddy." The man holds his hands out, as though he might soothe the beast. "Settle down." The man looks at me, a bit frantic.

I hold my breath as the deer rams its antlers right into the camera lens.

"What the hell?" The man turns and starts running for a car parked down the road near the bend. I hadn't noticed the car before. I might not have stopped if I did. The deer chases after him, with the black, shiny camera wobbling on the tip of its right antler. Little pieces of plastic fall to the ground as the deer runs. I take this moment to cross the road, get in my car, and get the hell out of there.

April 27, 2011

My mother called today and said she has some things for me. I haven't been to Newburgh in years. My parents are usually traveling, and there's nothing in Newburgh except memories of my dead sister.

As I drive to my childhood home, the sky threatens another thunderstorm, and it all feels a bit ominous. I follow the Hudson River, the road leading me to a moderately sized colonial, to a cul-de-sac on the outskirts of the city.

It helped being in a suburban area when Tori died. While the reporters were searching for pictures and stories and declarations from her friends, the county sheriff was nice enough to block the end of our street and keep the place quiet.

I pull up in front of the pale yellow house, get out, and knock on the door.

Dad opens it right away. "Hey, girlie." He steps out onto the porch to hug me. "You don't need to knock here. This is your home."

"Sure, Dad." I hug him back.

And just like clockwork, my mother's footsteps echo in the hallway. She butts in and pulls us apart. She's always done this, even when I was a child. She would take me away or take him away, interrupting any time we had together. It was like she didn't want my father to shower me with any of his affections.

"Hi, Mom."

"You're here. Finally." She kisses both of my cheeks.

"I came as soon as you called. I couldn't get here any faster."

"Oh, well." She takes my hand and pulls me into the house. "We just got back from the city. You know how everything moves so fast down there."

I was expecting her to say something about my weight loss, since she was always making remarks about how fat I was. She barely even notices that I'm half the size I was before. I glance back at Dad, and he rolls his eyes.

"Don't you just love the buzz of the city?" She doesn't give me a chance to answer before she pulls me into the dining room. "Okay." She lets out a breath. "Here it is," she says, stepping to the side like Vanna White.

I focus on the seven boxes in the middle of the floor. "What is this?" I ask.

"Oh, you know," she says lightly. "Just your things."

"What things?" I move toward the box on top and open its flaps. Inside I find a white and yellow picture book, a pair of tiny booties, and a small gown. I move to the next box and open it to find my elementary school pictures, projects, and artwork. I move on to another and find things from high school. In another I find photos from my wedding to Alex.

"Mom, what is all this?" I turn to find my father standing in the threshold between the dining room and the kitchen, looking awfully embarrassed. He shrugs and mouths "sorry."

"Well, it's just your things. I thought you could enjoy them at home since we're hardly ever here anymore."

I am the unwanted one. Still. Maximum ache starts rearing its ugly head.

"Mom . . ." I can't seem to find any words to say to her. Instead, I leave the dining room and head to the living room. I check the mantel over the fireplace, which once held a photo of me and Alex. It's gone. I scan the walls. All of the pictures of me are gone. There are only paintings and landscape photos from their travels.

I head to the stairwell and as I'm passing through the hall, I hear my mother's voice tell my father to bring the boxes to my car. All the pictures of me are gone from the walls; the only one left is of Tori, looking like a supermodel in her prom dress. It was yellow. I remember it now. Tori wore a canary yellow dress to her prom, and she looked like Miss America in it.

I run down the stairs and search for my mother, finding her in the kitchen, setting a teapot on the stove.

"You took down all of my pictures."

"Of course I did." She sounds lighthearted as she speaks, like it's no big deal.

"*All* of my pictures."

"And . . . ?"

"You left the one of Tori. Why would you take down all of *my* pictures and leave hers?"

In that second it's like a switch flips in my mother. Her shoulders stiffen; her voice drops a few tones. "I can't get rid of Tori's picture."

"Well, why would you get rid of all of mine?"

She steps toward me. The wrinkles on her face seem to deepen with her anger. "You can't just end it, can you? I can't take her things down. She is dead, Morgan. Tori is dead!"

"I know she's dead."

"You act like it didn't just happen. You've always been so jealous of her. Why can't you just get over the fact that she was better? We loved her, you know. She was my first-born. And you—"

What in the hell? All I can do is stare at her with an open mouth.

"Hey . . . hey . . ." My father steps into the kitchen. "Sweetie." His hands grip my mother's shoulders. "Sweetie, settle down. Hey . . ." He ducks his head to her level. "Look at me. Okay, you're going to have some tea and then you're going to take a nap."

The switch flips in my mother again. "I'm going to have tea?" She turns around, facing the stove.

"Yes," my father says. "Tea and then a nap." He turns to me and I notice a single bead of sweat dripping down his forehead. "Tea and then a nap," he repeats.

"I think . . ." my mother says, "I think I'll skip the tea and take the nap. I think I need the nap."

Pressing his lips together, he leads my mother out of the kitchen and brings her upstairs.

I swallow hard to try and stop the tears that are threatening. What the hell just happened? My mother has been a bit off, but she has never said something so cruel to my face.

"Sorry about that." My father walks back into the kitchen.

"What was that all about?" I ask, trying to ignore the ache in my chest. I always knew, deep down, but hearing her say those words.

"Girlie, there's something I need to talk to you about."

"Wha—"

"You're mother's sick." The words exit my father's mouth in a hurried rush, like he's been holding it in for way too long and always meant to tell me.

"Sick?"

"It's something she's been dealing with for as long as I've known her. She's supposed to take medicine, but sometimes she doesn't and she acts like this. It's been getting worse and worse. She takes her meds when we're on vacation, and then she forgets when we get home." He sighs. "Just . . . take your things . . . before something happens to them here." He steps forward, envelopes me in a warm hug, and holds me for longer than he's ever been allowed to by my mother. "I'm sorry."

"I . . ." I think for a second.

"I'm sorry she said those things. She's not herself when she's like this."

It makes me wonder when she is truly herself. Was she herself when I was a child? Was she herself after Tori died and she acted like I didn't exist? Was she herself when she didn't even show up for my college graduation because she was on another trip?

"I have to take her to the doctor, but you know how she is. She doesn't like doctors."

"Is she bipolar or something? Or is it dementia or Alzheimer's?"

"Years ago they said bipolar. But she does so well when we're traveling. It's like she's a different person. She thinks she doesn't need to take the pills." My father looks at his feet, embarrassed and uncomfortable. He should know better than to keep these things from me. I'm a nurse, for god's sake.

I try to put on my strong face, the one I've been practicing for years. "You should take her. They make new medications to help all of those conditions. Maybe she needs one of the newer versions."

"I'm sure." I feel his heavy hands on my shoulders. "She didn't mean it, you know."

"What's that?" I ask.

"What she said about Tori."

Tori.

Tori.

Tori.

When he says her name, I can see it on his face too. He may not have chosen a favorite like my mother did, but Tori's death—it's like it barely matters that I'm still alive.

"It's fine." I focus on the empty space in the dining room where there was a pile of boxes with my childhood in them. Now they're in my car. "I should go."

"Sure." He hugs me tight. "Love you, girlie." He kisses the top of my head.

"Love you too, Dad."

I drive home with my life in my trunk, the entire way trying to sort it all out. I'm sad that Tori died, I'm jealous that my parents love her more, and I ache at the fact that I will never get to know who my sister turned out to be. Just because we weren't close as children doesn't mean that we wouldn't have grown closer with age.

When I get home I carry the boxes inside, one by one, and set them in the spare bedroom. I pull out the picture of me and Alex, carry it downstairs, and put it in my workbag.

That night, as I'm driving to work, I pull over on the side of the road where Alex died, and I set the picture next to the white cross someone left there. Hearing a stick snap, I look into the surrounding woods and see the shadow of a deer standing there in the fading light. I count its antler tips. There are eight. An eight-point buck, just like the one that killed Alex. Just like the one that chased that cameraman away. I remind myself that I hate deer. If I had something to throw at it, I would have.

September 27, 2011

For the one-year anniversary of my husband's death, I figure, what the hell? I might as well drown myself in work instead of mope around at home. So here I am. I signed up for a double shift.

Cynthia gives me that look when I walk through the door. "Second warning," she mutters in my direction. "You'll crumble from the inside."

I ignore her.

The waiting room is packed and I spend my night in triage, asking people why they're here. I like to think of it as the front line of the battlefield. Triage gets coughed on first, bled on first, puked on first, spit at first, and sworn at first. I think Cynthia assigned me here for the full sixteen hours as punishment for not taking her advice to request more time off.

There is a college kid in the waiting room, I call him up just before midnight.

"Hey, I just saw you on the TV out there," he says, jerking his thumb toward the waiting room.

"Wasn't me." I shake my head.

I hate that strangers can make me feel so vulnerable. It's none of their business. Even if they *liked* the story on Facebook, that doesn't make them my friend or my family. That doesn't mean I'm going to tell them anything about my personal life. I wish I could remember how many years the news reports continued bringing up Tori's death and the pictures of her car accident. The school district had contacted my parents about using her story as an antidrinking campaign for prom night. They said no. But that didn't stop the news stations from doing it.

"Can you tell me why you're here today?" Maybe it's the firmness of my voice, but he gives a quick smirk, like he knows I'm lying.

"No. It was you." He points at me.

Punk.

"Mister . . ." I check his sheet to find out what his name is. "Sullivan." Wait, my last name's Sullivan. No biggie, it's a common name around here. "Could you please tell me what brings you to the emergency room tonight?" He's making a scene and the others that are waiting their turn in the triage hot seat are watching us. A man and woman dressed way too trendy for this area stand and make their way toward us. Wearing jewelry, designer clothes, and expensive shoes, they look like they're from the city. Maybe this is their son, and he's in college. I don't know. I don't care. I just want this kid to shut up and stop talking about the news flashing my dead husband's story with images of me all over the screen.

I look up at them from my chair. "Can I help you?"

The woman stares at me for half a second before speaking. "My son here . . ." The woman motions to the young man sitting in front of me. "He's been feeling sick for about a year now. Since his brother died."

"What are his symptoms?"

"Well . . ." She bites her lip and looks to the man who's standing next to her.

I wait.

"Headaches," the kid says.

An ER visit for headaches. Awesome. I take down the kid's details and a set of vital signs.

"You're her," the kid says as he stands to go back to the waiting room to wait his turn.

The husband looks bored; the wife, a bit pale and nervous. The kid stalks off toward the doors. I get the feeling that something else is going on here, but I'm not sure what. They're probably some family that Facebooked and tweeted and discussed the horrors of my tragedy across their dinner table.

"Sorry," the lady says. "It's his headaches. They make him a bit ornery."

"Sure." I gather my sheets and prep the kid's chart.

"Ask her about the money," the man mumbles to his wife.

"Excuse me?" I jerk upright. I tell myself he must be worried about the hospital bill.

The man gives me a firm look, like I took something that was his.

"Oh." The woman shoos her husband and touches her cheek. "Don't mind him. You know how men can be."

I force a tiny laugh. A fake laugh. No, not really. Alex was never that way. He was patient and caring and loving. He didn't care about money. "If you're worried about the bill, the hospital will bill your insurance first. Just bring the card to the registration clerk when she calls your name."

"I think it's her," the wife whispers to her husband.

"Ask her," the man mumbles.

That's it. I am so sick of people beating around the bush—watching the news and eyeballing me.

"Ask me what?" It comes out loud and snotty. The woman takes a step back.

"Morgan," the charge nurse snaps at me. "Come here."

Great, she must've heard. I leave the kid's parents standing in the triage area and head for the desk.

"Yes, Cynthia?" I ask.

Of all the people in this place, I like her the best. She has a sense of humor, she's always smiling, and she has faith—something I wish I had a bit more of. Maybe if God could have surprised another family with me, one that wanted me, maybe then I'd have a little more faith. Or if my sister and my husband lived, then I'd have faith. Then I wouldn't be so . . . so . . . bitter. Shit.

"Those people giving you a problem?"

Moment of truth. Admit they're trying to *out* me on the anniversary of my husband's death or suck it up and continue on with my shift.

"No," I tell her. "It's nothing I can't handle."

She looks at me over the top of her glasses, then down at the assignment sheet in front of her. "We're overstaffed tonight. And since you're overtime, I have to send you home."

"Can't someone else go?" I catch the television screen in the waiting room flash my husband's picture with a warning for motorcycle safety, because the deer begin moving in the cool weather.

Cynthia sighs. "We have a union and rules. Overtime people go home. I'm sorry."

She's not sorry. I know it. Cynthia doesn't want me here; she thinks I need to be home with family on the one-year anniversary. But I have no one to go home to.

I finish up my charting, give report, and clock out. As I'm making my way across the poorly lit parking lot to my car, I notice a dark SUV trailing me. So I walk a little faster and hear the quiet humming sound of a car window rolling down.

"Morgan," a feminine voice calls after me.

I turn. The SUV stops and the woman from the ER gets out. I can see her husband behind the wheel and a shadow in the backseat. It must be her son.

"You're name is Morgan, right?" she asks again as she gets closer to me.

"Yes," I answer.

"I'm Natasha Sullivan." She holds her hand out. "Alex's mother."

I stand still and focus on her face. After a few moments, I recognize the cleft in her chin, the high cheekbones, the soft brown eyes flecked with green. She looks so much like him; I don't know how I didn't notice before. I shake her hand.

"He never told me about you." I cross my arms after she releases my hand.

"He wouldn't." She swipes at a lock of hair and tucks it behind her ear. A giant glinting diamond stud winks at me from her earlobe. "He didn't leave us on good terms."

"He never said anything to me. Actually, he told me his parents were dead," I say.

Natasha's bottom lip quivers, and she reaches into her purse, pulling out a cigarette and a lighter. She brings the cigarette to her lips, lights it, and sucks in a deep breath. After she exhales a string of smoke, she says, "Alex may have thought of us as dead, but we have missed him." She looks around. "I see he found everything he wanted."

"What do you mean?"

"Alex had this dream. He called it his American dream. He didn't want anything we had to offer. Just a simpler life. A place to make a meager living, a small house in the suburbs, an ... average wife." She glances sideways at me before coughing out a laugh. "We gave him a BMW sports car for his sixteenth birthday. You know what he did with it? He traded it in for an old rusty truck. Then he pocketed the rest of the money." She pauses to take another drag off of her cigarette. "We gave him the best of everything— clothes, cars, places to live, an Ivy League education. Did he tell you he graduated with honors from the business school at Cornell?"

I shake my head no.

"He did. With a minor in fitness. And then you know what he did? He cut all contact with us. Said he wanted to make a name for himself. There something not right about that boy. Just like his father always said."

In that moment I realize, from the tone of Natasha's voice, she speaks about Alex the same way my mother speaks to me. I get the feeling that Alex's own mother didn't quite love him, not unlike my mother toward me. All that time I was married to a man who knew exactly how I felt. I thought I was the only unwanted one, but I was wrong. Alex was an unwanted one also.

"Lawyers told us he left the trust fund to you," Natasha says. "My husband's not very happy about that. It's a lot of money."

"I know," I tell her. "I haven't touched a penny of it. I didn't marry Alex for his money. He never told me about it. I didn't even find out about it until after he died."

"Hm." She takes another drag off of her cigarette. "You should use it, get your hair done, buy a new car, make yourself look . . . better. Like your sister."

"What did you just say?" I cannot control the snapping tone of my voice.

She smirks. "We watch the news. That story made national television, just like Alex's death. It's a pity, really. Life shitting on you like this."

What a bitch. No wonder Alex split with these people.

"At least you tried to save him. We watched the videos on YouTube. Could tell by the look on your face that you loved him. Tragic." She glances back at the SUV. "My husband wouldn't do that for me if I were lying in that road. That's what money and greed have done to him. I think Alex was afraid of turning out like his father. So as a mother, I thank you for trying to save him." She drops the cigarette to the pavement and twists her foot over it. Reaching into her purse again, she pulls out a small business card and hands it to me. "Any chance you had a child with him?"

"No." I take the card from her.

"Too bad. He always talked about having a houseful of kids."

My chest burns. The horn beeps on the SUV, and Natasha's husband makes an impatient gesture.

"It was nice to meet you, Morgan." Natasha steps forward and hugs me. I don't hug her back; instead, I stand there with my arms stiff at my sides, clenching my fists. As she's patting my back, she whispers in my ear, "I expect his soul will return as some elegant creature. His father will tell you it's bullshit, but I'm quite certain my mother came back as a hummingbird. You wouldn't believe it—a hummingbird perched on the kitchen window in the middle of New York City." She pulls away with a shrug of her delicate shoulders. "Good luck to you." She motions to the card. "Call me if you figure out what he comes back as. I'd like to know."

It seems just as my mother is a bit granola and bipolar, this woman believes in reincarnation and the supernatural. Must be all those double skinny mocha lattes and smog she's been ingesting her whole life.

Natasha gets in the SUV and they pull away. I look at the card in my hand. One side has an embossed logo that says Sullivan Enterprises; the other side has elegant handwriting with a phone number and e-mail address.

~

When I get home, I throw my workbag on the floor and sift through the stack of mail on my dining room table. There are three envelopes from the trust fund company. I open one out of curiosity. Since I've done nothing with the money, it just seems to gain interest and grow. I don't know what to do with it. I don't want it. My eyes scan way too many numbers under the column marked "Balance." It's overwhelming.

Unable to get the conversation with Natasha out of my head, I file away the mail then change into sweats and my new pair of running sneakers. Usually I stop at the park after the first three miles, but since tonight is special, I loop around the block and run for another three miles. By the time I make it back to the park, I'm too exhausted to think. I drop down on a bench, tilt my head back, and stare into the night.

The sky is clear and a billion billion billion stars twinkle down at me. I focus on the largest. I think it's actually Saturn or something, but I pretend it is Alex twinkling down at me from the heavens. And I pretend he has been reincarnated as a star and his twinkles are words and they're telling me things like *I love you* and *I miss you* and *I'm sorry I never told you I was independently wealthy*. Closing my eyes, I purse my lips into the night sky and kiss his star in the distant heavens.

Tears sting my eyes as I sit alone in the dark. I think about my mother's words and Cynthia's words, and I wonder if I'm already rotting inside. I must be. That's why I'm already a tiny bit bitter.

I can handle this.

I think I can handle this.

I can handle this, right?

It's just another hurdle to get over.

My mother went to the Cayman Islands this week and dragged my father there. When she told me she was going, Dad gave me a sheepish look. He knows she can't look at me for more than thirty minutes, not after her second favorite person on earth died in a horrific accident. I wonder if coping would be easier if she were here with me. Maybe she could hold me in her arms, stroke my hair, and whisper things in my ear like *It's going to be okay* or *they're in a better place* or *we still have each other*. Instead, I'm staring at the starry night alone, thinking about the sister I will never get to know better and the husband I will never grow old with.

It seems even in my adulthood I am the unwanted one, the unexpected one, the not-Tori and the not-Alex. It's a lonely existence being plain and invisible. Maybe I should go to the salon like Natasha suggested. Even with my natural brown hair, I wasn't invisible to Alex. I was his twinkly star that he sought out from the hundreds of other women that walked through the doors of his gym. It seems I have only ever twinkled for him, though. Not for my mother, his mother, or any other guy. I wish I could just let it all go and be free.

November 5, 2011

Exactly one year from when Mr. Peterson informed me that I was a partner in my deceased husband's gym, I received the first notice. "Past Due" was stamped on the front of the envelope. Knowing that all of my bills were paid, I ignored it. A week later another one showed up. And then another. And another. They kept coming. Addressed to me. And then the bank called.

After finding out the reason for the letters, I didn't bother calling Nick. I marched my ass down to the gym after work one morning. I waited in my car as the sun rose and watched as Nick pulled in the parking lot, his truck glinting in the sunlight like Alex's star glinted in the darkness. He went inside, and I gave him five minutes before I got out and went in after him.

I forgot how it smells like disinfectant and rubber mats in here.

"We're not open yet," Nick shouts from the back office.

"I know," I shout back.

Nick leaves the back and freezes when his eyes fall on me. Nick doesn't say anything. I haven't seen him in almost a year. Not since Alex died and he showed up with Mr. Peterson. He was at the funeral, hiding in the corners of the room, and said nothing to me. Typical.

But right now Nick should be shocked, or barely recognize me. For god's sake, I let my hair grow past my shoulder blades for the first time ever, and my thighs don't even rub together anymore. Instead, Nick's eyes fall on me as though he's looked at me every day for the past year; there's no surprise, only recognition that I'm here, but am usually not. Good thing I'm used to being the unexpected one. I'm used to the look; it doesn't faze me. And yet, a moment of guilt surges through me as I realize that over the past year I should have done something to be involved. I did refuse to sell my share to Nick, and then I left everything for him to take care of alone.

I hold up the stack of overdue bills.

"Why didn't you contact me?" I ask.

"I didn't need to contact you." His voice comes out like gravel.

"I think you do." I throw the bills down on the front counter. "I'm still part owner in this gym."

"And I have been trying to buy your share for over a year."

I stare back at him. Mr. Peterson only mentioned it to me the one time.

"Why won't you sell?" Nick walks toward me—he's huge and intimidating—and standing this close to him, I can see why they call him The Strangler. He looks like he's ready to strangle me.

"I don't want to sell." Standing my ground, I drop my bag onto the counter and dig for my checkbook.

"Why not?" he asks.

What do I tell him? I can't sell because this is the last connection I have to my dead husband? No, that will make me look stupid. Ignoring his question and finding my checkbook in the depths of my bag, I pull it out and open to a new check.

"How much do you need?" I ask.

"I don't need your money."

I motion to the stack of overdue bills. "Of course you don't. Seems to me like you've got it all under control."

Nick makes a scoffing noise. "I don't need your money." I try to ignore the muscles bulging in his neck and shoulders as he crosses his arms.

"Look at the shirt you're wearing right now." He gives me a look of *seriously?* But he glances down at his shirt. "Yeah, you see that there, buddy? That's my last name sprawled across your rock-hard pecs." I start writing a check. I make it out to him, but I can't remember his last name. "What's your last name?" I ask.

He hesitates. "I don't need your money."

"Neither do I. What's your last name, Nick? For some stupid reason I can't remember it right now."

"Stacks."

That's right. Nick "The Strangler" Stacks. I make it out to him, pausing only to point the end of my pen at the stack of bills. "That's almost seven thousand dollars. How much else do you need?"

"I don't need your money."

"It's not my money." I start filling out the date. "Now, tell me how much more you need."

He shakes his head, and I ignore the way his blond hair brushes across his forehead. "I—"

"I'll just round it up to ten." I finish writing the check for ten thousand dollars, rip it out of the checkbook, and set it on the stack of bills.

"I don't need you here. Keep your money."

"It's not my money," I remind him.

"Whose money is it?" he asks, annoyed.

I toss the checkbook back in my bag. "It's Alex's insurance money."

Nick freezes still, his jaw twitching. For one second I make eye contact. His eyes are blue. I never noticed before and seeing the watery gleam there right now, I wish I hadn't looked. I'm sure my eyes look the same. I take my bag, fling it onto my shoulder, and get ready to turn away from him.

Just before my hands hit the cool metal of the front door, Nick says, "I just didn't want to worry you." His voice is so low and deep, I barely hear his words.

"Then don't worry me. Cash the check. Pay the bills."

"Thanks."

I leave, head to my car, and go home. I transfer the money to cover the check before taking a hot shower and falling into a mindless sleep.

When I wake up, it's evening. This is the downfall of nightshift work. While the rest of the world is sleeping, you're awake. I change into a pair of yoga pants and a long sleeve T-shirt and twist my hair up into a bun. Then I do the same thing I've done every night I haven't had to work. I lace up my sneakers, leave my house, and leap off of my porch like I'm twelve years old again, and as soon as my feet hit the cement of the sidewalk, I take off running.

This is what I do now. I run until the burning in my chest is stronger than the pain I feel from losing Alex. Even a year later I can barely stand the strength of it. And in those few minutes in which I can no longer bear the pain, my body numbs and I am free. I can let him go. I drown myself in maximum ache and let it swallow me whole and spit me out like a piece of overchewed gum. It still hurts like a bitch.

Afterward, there's always a surge when the sadness comes back, and it is always worse. Lying in the grass, I roll to my side and make a sound that's halfway between a hiccup and a strong sob, hating this part. When I hear the crunching sound of dried leaves being stepped on, I jerk upright.

"Morgan?" a deep voice asks. I recognize the voice instantly; I spoke to the person who it came from this morning.

Scrambling to sit and wiping at my face, I ask, "Nick? What're you doing out here?"

He comes into view, out of the shadows of the tall oaks that line the street. He's wearing a sweat-soaked shirt, a pair of shorts, and running shoes. Just like me.

"I could ask you the same thing, but I think I know."

You already know I'm sobbing in the grass like a total basket case? Wonderful.

Nick holds out his hand. I stare at it for a moment, unsure of what to do. No one has offered to scrape me off the ground before. I reach for him, scrambling like a fool, afraid he's going to turn all jerk on me. His large hand engulfs mine as he pulls me to my feet. The first thing I think when his skin touches mine is how warm his hand is, like a cozy fire I want to curl up next to.

Standing and wiping my sweaty palms on my pants, I ask, "So what are you really doing out here?"

The fall wind blows his hair around as he looks everywhere but at me. "Running."

"Hm."

"You know, you shouldn't be out here alone at night."

"There are less than ten thousand people in New Paltz. I bet we're the only two people out here right now. It's fine."

"I know how many people live here," he replies.

"I'm not scared of the dark." What would I do without my nighttime runs? They are the only thing keeping me from totally cracking. That and work.

"This is still a college town. And sometimes the hoodlums wander off of campus," Nick warns.

I would like to laugh in his face. Why would a college kid bother me? There's no reason. I'm pushing thirty and . . . used. In the world of shiny new BMWs, I'm a rusty Chrysler LeBaron.

"I'll take my chances." I lean to the side to stretch my burning leg muscles. "What are you doing here, really? Last I knew you lived two towns over." He's always lived closer to the gym and closer to the city so he didn't have to travel so far for his fights.

"Moved. Last year."

"Oh." I straighten and rest my hands on my waist. "Where do you live now?" I ask.

"Nearby."

He probably lives with his mom. Like a serial killer. A true strangler.

I don't push him, because I seriously don't care much where he lives. "Well." I look up at the full moon. "I should head home."

"I'll go with you," he offers.

I try to hide my surprise. I've never met Chivalrous Nick. "If you can keep up," I joke.

He can do laps around me. I'm pretty sure.

Nick keeps up, jogging annoyingly at my side, perfect pace, until we reach my house three miles later. There's something unnerving having The Strangler jogging next to you. I stop to catch my breath, walking in wide circles on the sidewalk in front of my house. I doubt that he's as winded as I am right now.

"Thanks."

He nods.

"Okay."

Things are awkward as he says nothing, but the tension in the air is telling me he wants to say something.

"Bye," I say with a wave.

He nods again.

I go inside, lock the door behind me, and watch through the small window in the front door. Nick's still there, watching the door I just walked through. After a few minutes he shakes his head and runs up the street.

November 6, 2011

The next day it starts snowing. Since winter has arrived, I head down to the local twenty-four-hour gym and sign up for a membership. At least I can run here each night, instead of freezing my butt off in the cold. As I'm signing the paperwork at the front desk, I think to myself, *This is so stupid. I own a gym.* But, I realize that while I may be a partner in it, I'm not welcome there. And I can't deal with Nick.

"Mrs. Sullivan." An old man's voice begs me to turn around and when I do, Mr. Peterson stands there wearing a pair of *awesome* gym shorts. They are entirely too short and obnoxiously orange.

"Hello." I smile at him and finish signing my name.

He walks toward me and asks, "What are you doing here? You own a gym."

The lady behind the desk gives me a questioning look, her eyebrows all furrowed.

"Well . . . I . . . I just . . ." I set the pen down and slide the papers back to the desk lady. "I can't go there."

"Well." He chuckles like I'm being ridiculous. "Why not?"

"I just can't."

He settles a hand on my elbow. "You should try." His voice drops to a whisper. And while the desk lady shuffles my papers, I notice her watching us out of the corner of her eye. "It's not that I don't want you supporting our local gym, but you own one. You have a business to run. It's important. You have to build a business up. Be its Ark or it will topple."

Does everyone around here use *Ark* as a metaphor?

"It's doing just fine without me," I assure him.

Mr. Peterson smiles this gentlemanly smile, and his eyes glint with mischief. "Doing just fine, you say?"

"Uh-huh."

He moves closer and pats my hand. "Maybe you should swing on over there and talk with that nice young man. What's his name? Nicky?"

"Nick. *The Strangler.*" I add that last part for effect.

"Yes. That's right. I heard he lost his last fight."

"That's too bad."

Peterson pats my hand again. "Maybe you should stop on down there."

Yeah, I could stop on down there. But I'm not sure if I can handle more than five minutes standing in the gym that Alex spent almost every day of his life in.

The town gym does not have grass or darkness or stars. It has bright fluorescent lights, textured carpeting, and spiders in the corners of the ceiling. And mirrors. There's like a million mirrors in this place. It smells like watered-down disinfectant that wouldn't kill a single germ. I don't touch the other equipment, just the treadmill.

I'd rather be outside. But the New York winters are cold and long. It even keeps people out of the emergency room, which means I don't get to pick up overtime. My mother and father travel to Europe, China, and Japan. From the messages and the phone calls, my mother sounds a bit more stable, but she usually is when she's traveling. There was never any more talk of the day she packed up my life and handed it over to me in seven cardboard boxes. It seems she was ridding herself of the unwanted. I didn't even expect any phone calls while she was gone.

I wonder if I had died instead of Tori, would she save my picture at the top of the stairs?

At least twice a week, Alex comes to me in my dreams. I guess that's what happens when you're dreaming with a broken heart. Everyone you love and miss shows up and taunts you in every form but live-human.

Cynthia gives me looks when I walk into work for the few overtime shifts that are available. She gives me my third, fourth, and fifth warnings. She knows I still have no Ark, and she doesn't approve.

Some new people move in next door to me. It's a giant house. Twice the size of mine. I've always had house envy for it and anyone who's lived in it. Currently it's a pair of empty nesters, a man and woman in their forties. The woman looks overly tanned with perfectly highlighted hair, and the man is fit and tall with a mop of black hair that needs to be cut. On sunny mornings they sit on their back deck, which overlooks my little yard, and sip orange juice while working on their laptops, like they're rich or something with their big sunglasses on. They sit there just for an hour or so until the winter chill seems to knock some sense into them, and they go inside for the rest of the day.

Part of me thinks they sit out there because they're snooping. I avoid them.

The strangest thing is, all winter long I find these odd animal tracks on my lawn. They look like upside-down hearts. If I had a desire to get my laptop out, I would look them up. But the dreaded *#foreveryoung* keeps me from doing so.

April 1, 2012

As soon as the snow melts and the spring air hits, I ditch the bright, barely clean-smelling gym and embrace my night. I run my three miles straight to the town park, just like I did before winter.

As I slow to view the stars, I hear footsteps behind me. Heavy footsteps, like an ox is running down the sidewalk. Turning, a large form is running toward me. I backstep and a scream forms in my throat just as I trip and fall backward onto the soft, muddy earth.

"Morgan, it's me. Nick."

Nothing will scare the shit out of you like having Nick "The Strangler" run up behind you in the middle of the night.

"Holy shit." I collapse on the ground, regretting it instantly when I feel my bun sinking into the mud as my head hits the ground.

"I told you last fall that you shouldn't be out here alone." Nick rests his hands on his hips and looks down at me. He's huge—giant—with muscles bulging in his arms and legs. The sweat dripping down his face and arms glistens in the moonlight. All he needs is a black mask and some rope. Then he'd definitely look the part of The Strangler.

"I know." I force my mouth to move. "I'm fine."

Nick holds a hand out. This time I don't hesitate; I grasp it and let him pull me to my feet. His hand is just as warm as it was the last time.

"Sorry I scared you," he says.

I test my hair for mud. "I wasn't scared." Yup, there's mud in my hair, and it isn't going to come out without a shower. I wipe my hands on my shorts.

"You screamed like a chicken."

"Chickens don't scream, they cluck," I correct him.

"Sure." He turns a bit and looks around. In the hazy glow of the moon, I notice his blond hair is a bit shaggy and long, and there are bruises and scrapes on his face.

"What happened to you?" I ask. "You're damaged."

One of his hands moves to a cut near his lip. "Had a fight this past weekend."

"Oh." I remember the fight I went to a couple of years ago and the brutality of it. I wouldn't think a fighter like Nick would be out running two days later. For some reason I always envisioned him bedridden for a few weeks afterward, maybe in a full body cast, getting IV fluids. That's how I think MMA fighters recover, after witnessing them in action.

"Did you win?" I ask.

"I almost always win." He says it like I should know.

"Did you get that looked at?" I ask, motioning to his busted face.

"Yeah. You take self-defense classes or anything?" He changes the subject.

"No. Why would I need to?"

"Because you're out running in the night. Alone."

"It's fine."

"It's not."

I give up arguing with The Strangler and sigh in defeat.

"How about I run with you?" He says it so blandly, like it's a chore. Here, how about I run with you and it will be just another task on my to-do list, like cleaning the kitchen or emptying the litter pan or taking out the garbage or strangling people in the Octagon.

I am tired of people. "No deal," I reply. "Goodnight." I turn and start to jog home.

Hearing footfalls behind me, I turn my head just slightly and see Nick trailing me. "I don't need you to follow me," I shout over my shoulder, instantly wishing I hadn't, when the curtains flutter in the front windows of a nearby house. Great. They'll be on their porch or calling Peterson in the morning to complain about the noise.

Running as fast as I can, and I'm sure looking like an idiot in the process, I make it home in record time. Nick just runs past me without a word.

"I don't need you," I mutter after him.

The next day, I open my car door to find a can of pepper spray on my driver's seat and a barely legible note that, I think, reads "You should lock your car doors."

June 29, 2012

Nick trails me all spring and summer long. As I run, I grip the pepper spray in my hand and pretend I don't see him. I was alone for most of my life before Alex came along, and it never bothered me. But now, having Nick "The Strangler" following me at night, it's a bit frightening. Sometimes I don't notice him, and he scares the shit out of me, then I rip into him about how it's not nice to scare the shit out of a person in the middle of the night when they're trying to run. It puts a real damper on my stamina.

When I get home, sometimes I say thanks; he usually just waves and continues on to wherever he lives. Every so often I think that maybe I'll work up the courage to speak to him. But I have nothing to say, and he's very intimidating, and I don't think he even wants to talk to me. It makes me wonder why he bothers following me. Maybe he's bored.

Since Alex is gone, I have to do things myself now, like mow the lawn. That's what today is dedicated to. Each time I start the lawn mower, the new neighbors look at me like I've interrupted their vacation. So sometimes I mow the back lawn twice. It's payback for all the times they mow their lawn while I'm sleeping between night shifts. There's nothing more annoying than being woken up at noon to the sound of a riding mower and Weedwacker and leaf blower, and knowing that you have to go back to work in six short hours.

"Hey! Hey!" a voice shouts as I mow along the property border.

I pull out my earbuds and stop the mower. Turning around, I find my new neighbor standing in my yard.

I wish I had a fence.

"Hi." He holds out his hand. "I don't think we've met formally. My name is Doug Richards." He turns and waves toward their deck. "And that's my wife. Michelle."

I shake his hand. "I'm Morgan."

"Yeah, we know."

He knows? Well, it's a small town, people talk. I wonder if they *liked* Alex's Facebook page?

"So, we were wondering, have you been having any trouble with the deer?"

What the hell? He has to know my husband was killed by a deer. I should tell him that I hate deer— that's my deep dark secret.

Doug turns and points toward a flower bed at the side of his house. "Something keeps eating our flowers. Michelle said she saw a deer out here a few nights in a row. Deer like the plants, right?"

"I have no idea," I say.

"It was a huge deer. Eight-pointer," Michelle shouts across the yard and moves her arms to indicate the size of the antlers on her own head.

"I haven't seen any deer," I say.

Michelle trots down the steps of their deck and makes her way to us. "Has it been eating your flowers also?"

Pointing to the front of my house, I say, "I don't have any flowers."

"Oh," Michelle gasps and holds her hand against her chest like she can't believe it, like it's a national tragedy that I can't be bothered to plant flowers in my front yard.

"Maybe you should plant some," Doug suggests. "Might brighten up the neighborhood."

"Sure. I've got lots of time for planting flowers," I mutter.

"What was that?" Doug asks.

"If there is a deer eating the flowers, it will just eat mine too," I say.

"I think we're going to put up a camera. Live feed. That way we can really see if it's a deer or something else."

I look between our houses. Without a fence or bushes, if they put up a camera, it's going to point directly at my house and my yard.

"I don't think you need a camera," I say.

"I think it's a good idea," Doug says. "Right there, on the corner of the deck. Maybe we could put a motion sensor on it. Or a light. Maybe a motion light would scare it off."

"How about you just put a motion light up and skip the camera," I offer.

"What's your problem with a camera?" Michelle asks.

"I like my privacy," I say, twisting the earbuds between my fingers. "If you have a camera focused on my yard—"

"It's not like we're going to do anything improper," Michelle scoffs.

"Sure." I press one earbud into my ear. I'm so over this discussion. "That's what the tabloids said when they hid in the bushes and took photos of me at my husband's grave and sold them to the highest bidder on the one-year anniversary of his accident."

"Oh, dear." Michelle's hand covers her mouth.

"I understand you've had some issues with the press, but that's not what we're trying to do here. We just want the deer to stop eating our flowers," Doug says. "I mean, hasn't it been almost two years since that accident? They can't still be doing stories on it."

"Just wait until September, Mr. Richards," I say as I press the other earbud into my ear. "Please don't put the camera up." I turn on my music and move to start the lawn mower again.

Doug and Michelle go back to their porch, and I finish mowing the lawn.

A camera. What the heck is wrong with people? Put up a fence or something. I glance around my yard. Maybe I'll put up a fence. I think about the cost. Maybe I won't put up a fence. I don't want to spend the money.

The thought of the trust fund enters my brain. I have more than enough money. I could just move. Sell this little house and get an apartment, so I don't have to worry about mowing the lawn, or being bothered by nosy neighbors or the deer. But then I'd have to worry about the noise, the parking, and the stomping from the apartment above mine while I'm trying to sleep. No, I won't sell the house. Along with the gym, it's all I have left of him. I can handle the Richardses.

As I put the mower in the garage, I stop and focus on the tarp-covered truck. It's been parked here since he died. My father covered it. He said Mom couldn't stand looking at the truck when she walked through my garage to get in the side door of my house. I flip up the corner of the heavy plastic covering. "Sullivan's Gym" is detailed over the hood with the image of an upper torso, the arms up, and biceps flexed. Since I can't bring myself to sell the truck, I should bring it down to the gym. Nick could drive it, or one of the other employees.

I wonder how many employees there are? I should know this. I'm part owner.

For the two-year anniversary of Alex's death, my mother took off to Cabo San Lucas. She will not hold me as I mourn. We will not bond over the deaths of our loved ones. Ever. This has become fact to me now. When she comes back, I know we won't speak of it. I'll ignore the fact that she runs away from death as I am left to face it, and that I am still the unwanted one even though I'm the only one left alive. And since she has already boxed up all my shit, she has me halfway out of her life already.

I don't bother scheduling myself for overtime. I don't even schedule myself to work. Instead, I order a cheese pizza and eat it all in one sitting, in silence, alone. I wash the pizza down with a beer. And then I throw it all up. There goes fourteen ninety-nine down the drain. I tell myself it's just because I'm not used to eating that much food in one sitting anymore. I haven't thrown up since I had the stomach bug four years ago.

Brushing my teeth afterward, I try to get rid of the taste of losing my dignity. At least I was alone.

Stepping out of the master bathroom, I wind up in the bedroom, looking at Alex's side of the bed. I still haven't washed the bedding. It's gross, I know. But sometimes I can still smell him on it. Like in the middle of the night when I wake up from dreaming about him or when it's hot and humid in the summer months. Somehow that seems to pull all the little molecules of his scent out of the pillow stuffing and I sniff it into my nose and remember him.

I miss him.

Collapsing on the bed, I press my face into the pillow and inhale. But there's nothing this time. An emptiness fills me. Disappointment. I don't cry. I swallow it down. Stand. Pull on a pair of running shorts and a long-sleeved shirt. When I get downstairs, I lace up my sneakers and run.

Six miles, just like last year. This time when I toss myself onto the park bench, I'm not as out of breath, but my stomach hurts. An empty stabbing void. I regret the pizza and the beer.

There was a time when I could eat half of a pizza by myself in one sitting. Those were the days. Gluttony at its best. Now I can't handle that much food. But, at least I don't have the love handles or the bulging stomach. I try to decide if it's worth it. Is it worth it? I'm still undecided. I didn't start running to lose weight; I started running so I could experience those few moments when grief and loss do not consume me, when maximum ache chews me up and spits me out anew.

When I tilt my head back and stare up, the sky is not clear and the billion billion billion stars that litter the space above earth do not twinkle down at me. How dare there be clouds on this night? All I wanted to do was blow a kiss at the twinkling Saturn and pretend it was Alex glinting down at me.

"Fuck you, heavens," I grumble into the darkness.

The crinkling sound of something stirring in the nearby forest startles me, and I sit up. Out steps a huge deer with a giant rack. Suddenly the clouds break and the eerie glow of the full moon shines down on the creature. It's like I'm watching *Bambi*. No, it's like I'm standing in the middle of *Bambi*. My eyes focus on the antlers, and I wonder how the animal can hold its head up with all that weight. There are eight tips, all reaching for the sky. An eight-point buck. Just like the deer I saw last year, but bigger, like it's grown and put on weight. And then the image of the dead deer flashes through my head, the gash in Alex's thigh. I hate that goddamned deer right now.

"I hate you!" I scream at the thing as I stand.

The buck tips its head to the side and focuses on me—of all the things for it to do. I hate that deer. I hate every deer that ever existed. I take the few steps to the rock path and pick up a brick the size of my palm.

"I hate you!" I scream as I throw the brick. It makes a soft thud as it lands nowhere near the deer. All the deer does is stare at me one last time before ambling back into the forest.

"Are you okay?" A deep voice scares me. I actually scream as I turn and stumble away. Nick is standing here, his hair damp and his shirt spotted with perspiration. He doesn't look the same as he has all summer while he's trailed me on my runs; he looks a bit . . . broken.

"You just scared the shit out of me." I cover my heart and feel it beating rapidly in my chest and try to compose myself in front of the man who just witnessed me screaming and throwing rocks at an innocent deer. "I have specifically asked you at least a hundred times not to scare the shit out of me at night."

"You just scared the shit out of that buck."

Great, he saw it. One dark brow rises, and I can't tell if it's in amusement or disgust.

"I don't care." I cross my arms and straighten my back to stand up a little taller so I don't feel so small next to him. I think he's a full foot taller than me. So he must be around six-three.

"You feeling all right?" He looks me up and down.

Of course I'm not feeling all right. He should know. He looks a little pale himself.

"Fine," I say.

"I don't think you are. You look . . . ill."

"I threw up earlier."

"Are you sick?"

"No. I ate an entire medium cheese pizza." Why the hell am I having a case of verbal diarrhea in the middle of the night with Nick, on *tonight* of all nights? "And I drank a beer."

Nick chuckles. For the first time ever I see his shoulders shudder, and he presses his lips together, holding in a smile. He's always so stoic. I just assumed his laughing muscles were all broken, or maybe he was born without them.

"It's not funny." I rub my neck. "My throat kinda hurts."

"If you're going to go on an eating binge, you need to start a few days before and stretch your stomach out."

I can't tell if he's being serious or messing with me.

Suddenly the mood turns dark, without any words being said.

"I know what today is," Nick finally says as he rubs his hand across his mouth.

"Me too."

"Did you watch the news?" he asks.

"Don't watch TV anymore. Can't even get on the computer."

"Me either."

The clouds break and the full moon illuminates the park. Nick's face is all shadows and darkness. I look up and search for the brightest star. Finally. The heavens will not deny me tonight of all nights. The stars twinkle down at me, and I try to remember the sound of Alex's voice, but I can't. My stomach drops and I feel ill again. More ill than when I ate that pizza.

Somehow, knowing, Nick moves and he's right there next to me, close.

I tip my face up at him, horrified at my latest revelation. "I can't remember the sound of his voice." I feel my jaw quiver, the telltale sign that an emotional breakdown is about to steamroll me.

Nick says nothing. Nick usually says nothing.

And then, that damned buck with the huge rack steps out of the cover of the trees again and looks right at us. I move quickly, picking up three bricks and chucking them at the animal, screaming at the top of my lungs "I hate you!"

"Why do you hate the deer?" Nick asks. "The deer that killed him died."

"If there were no deer in these parts, one would have never run in front of Alex as he drove his motorcycle to work that morning. He would have never died." My lack of faith is solidified once again (sorry Cynthia). If God had never created deer, my husband would have never died. It's just one vicious fucking circle.

This time the deer runs away after my outburst. I don't look at Nick. Instead I cross my arms tightly over my abdomen and say, "I miss him."

Nick spreads an arm behind my back. "Me too," he says.

I don't think much about it, Nick touching me like this. Since my mother and father are not here to comfort me, I'll take it where I can get it.

"I hate this," I say, my voice croaking.

"Just let it go, Morgan."

I shudder in his arms, knowing that we are not friends and not enemies; we are some strange state in between, drawn together by the one tragedy that has forever changed us. After vomiting and running and crying and verbally harassing a buck, I fall asleep sitting on the park bench, tucked tightly against Nick's side.

When I wake up, it's early morning. My butt is numb, and Nick's head is tipped away from me, his chin on his chest. Relaxed in sleep, his face looks so much younger and innocent. There's less anger, less coldness, less *Nick* to him. He no longer looks like

Nick "The Strangler"; he looks like a handsome young man. It doesn't matter that his nose is slightly crooked—probably from being broken in so many fights—or that he has a scar along his temple. He's nice to look at, now that he's down to my level.

The soft chatter of voices causes me to look away from Nick. The Sunday morning McDonald's gang is headed toward us: Bill, Jack, Buzz, and Peterson. I've seen them all there every Sunday when I stop to get coffee on my way home from work. All of them are carrying steaming Styrofoam cups of coffee.

Nick stirs and moves away from me, and I am instantly chilled to the bone. Mr. Peterson notices us and walks our way, with his gang of old farts following him. This is going to be awkward.

"Good morning, Morgan and Nick. Don't usually see you young ones out this early."

"Went out for an early run." I lie to him.

I see the way his eyes twinkle a bit at finding us together. Mr. Peterson doesn't want sad souls in his little town. He wants happiness and white picket fences tucked into the spaces among the Catskill Mountains. I think that's why he didn't badger me with Nick's requests for me to sell my share of the gym. Mr. Peterson knew it would drive me crazy.

"Good morning for it." He takes a deep breath and hitches his pants up a bit. "Mrs. Stevenson down the street said she heard someone yelling in the park in the middle of the night." His eyes flick between me and Nick. "Wouldn't know what that's all about, would you?"

"I never heard a thing," Nick says and he stands.

I stand too.

"Hm." Mr. Peterson looks at the stone path and kicks his foot around the missing bricks that I threw at that deer. "Looks like I'll need to get a crew out here to fix this."

Bill, Jack, and Buzz sip at their coffees and watch us like creepers. I guess it's a good thing, knowing all of your townspeople and having your thumb on the pulse of everything going on. But this morning I find it a bit annoying.

"Hear you've got another fight next week, Nick." Mr. Peterson looks away from the park path. "Your mother says it's a big one. Another title event."

Nick nods. "Yeah. Next weekend."

Mr. Peterson notices the third missing brick in the walkway, and his eyes flick to mine for a split second. I'm sure Alex told him I'm not into the fights. I don't run with that crowd. Actually, I guess I don't run with any crowd.

"Me and the boys here, we've been doing rounds. Seems there's been some damage to the walkway. Happens every few months or so. A brick goes missing. Usually Dave, the parks manager, he mows the grass out here. Seems he's hit a brick out there." He points to the far edge of the forest. "Busted a few blades. Been trying to figure out who's defacing the walkways. I don't like to see the townspeople's tax dollars thrown out the window." He clears his throat. "You seen anyone out here throwing the bricks?"

"Ah . . ." I'm at a loss for words. "No."

"Hm." Mr. Peterson sips at his coffee, seemingly deep in thought.

Nick says, "Well, I've promised to walk Morgan home." He moves toward me and, taking my elbow, he directs me away from the old men.

"Nice save," I mutter to him when we're far enough away not to be heard.

"Shh," Nick scolds me. "If they have their hearing aids turned up they'll hear you."

I laugh.

Nick chuckles. For the first time ever I see his shoulders shudder, and he presses his lips together, holding in a smile.

As we begin the three-mile walk to my house, Nick asks, "You want to get something to eat?"

I shake my head. "I feel pretty gross. I think I need a hot shower and a nap."

"Oh." His voice drops.

I tell myself that's not disappointment I hear in his voice. I tell myself it's relief. Why the hell would Nick want to spend one second longer with me than necessary?

"Peterson knows your mom?" I ask.

"Yeah. They play bingo together on Saturday nights."

"Nice."

"Not really," Nick says. "They're all kinda meddlesome."

I couldn't agree more with him. Alex and I settled here because Alex was certain the aging population would move on soon, and by the time we had kids, New Paltz would be filled with new families. Seems the old people aren't going far.

We stop in front of my house.

"Hey, Morgan!" a female voice shouts from next door. I turn to find Michelle standing on her deck, orange juice in hand, but this time it's in a freaking wine goblet. Who drinks orange juice like that? I wave back and notice that she's eyeing Nick like he's a piece of fresh meat.

"Who's that?" Nick asks.

"New neighbors. They moved in this past winter."

"Hm." He scratches his jaw. "What's that guy screwing into the deck railing?"

I turn to see Doug screwing down what looks like a small camera.

"Crap."

"What's wrong," Nick asks.

"A few weeks ago, they said a deer was eating their flowers. They said they wanted to put up a camera with a live feed to catch it."

"Doesn't sound so bad." Nick shrugs.

"I asked them not to."

"Why?"

"No better than the reporters."

Nick stiffens. He knows what I mean. "You want me to say something to them?" he asks.

"No." I turn to see Michelle still ogling Nick.

"Let me know if you do."

"What are you going to do, strangle them?" I ask.

He shrugs and makes a face like that's actually an option.

"Don't worry about it. I can take care of the meddlesome neighbors."

"Later," Nick says as he takes off jogging down the street.

I'm not sure where he found the energy, but I'm exhausted. My stomach grumbles loudly. Maybe I should have taken him up on his offer for breakfast.

October 9, 2012

"Did you see the shit in our yard?" Doug shouts across our invisible property boundaries.

"Why would I see anything in your yard?" I pull the mower out of the garage for one last trimming before winter.

"I think it's from that deer." He runs a hand over his chin. "I think that deer is shitting in our yard on purpose."

"Doug, it's a deer." Grabbing the gas can from near the garage door, I start filling the mower.

"It's like the thing is taunting me."

He has no clue. The deer taunt me, not him. The elusive eight-point buck. It killed my husband, then came back to haunt me. I have developed a bitter hatred for the deer in this town.

"Is there shit in *your* yard?" he asks.

I shrug. "I don't think so."

"Oh, hey, I don't see you much during the day. Why is that?" Doug changes the subject fast.

"Because I work nights." Putting the cap back on the gas can, I move to set it on the shelf in the garage.

"Oh, that's right."

I turn quick to face him. *That's right?* Has he been spying on me?

"I asked you not to put up that camera." I point to his deck. Michelle is sitting there, on her computer. She mistakes my point for a wave and waves back with a good-afternoon smile.

"It's not hurting you."

"Is it recording my property?" I ask.

"I'm not sure. Probably not."

"Make sure it doesn't." I pull the starter cable of the lawn mower, and it roars to life.

It sounds like he says something else to me, but over the sound of the mower I can't hear him.

By the time I'm done with the lawn, Doug and Michelle have graduated from afternoon coffee to margaritas.

"Oh, Morgan!" Michelle shouts in a singsong voice. "Want to come over for drinks?"

Sure, I want a margarita, I just don't want to be sipping it in their company. Then I think about the last time I interacted with real live people during the daytime. It's been a while. Maybe I should. I don't want to prove Cynthia right.

"Sure." I hold up my hands. "Just let me clean up a bit."

After taking a quick shower and changing into something socially acceptable that isn't scrubs or sweats, I search my kitchen for something to bring over to them. There's milk, coffee, and yogurt. Damn, none of this is acceptable. My focus settles on the saltshaker. *Ding.* Margaritas and salt. I grab the shaker and head on over.

As I cross into their yard, I start to get a bit nervous. I don't spend much time with other people. Especially people that tend to annoy me like these two do. Maybe if I spend some time with them, I can talk them into getting rid of the camera.

"Hey, Morgan." Michelle gives me a wide smile as I step up onto their deck.

I hold up the saltshaker. "Sorry, I didn't have much else to bring. Unless you wanted yogurt." I add a smile at the end.

"Don't worry about it." Doug stands and heads for the screen door. "I'll go make you a drink."

"He makes the best margaritas." Michelle raises her glass to me. I think she's already drunk. "So, who was that handsome man that you were walking with the other morning?"

"Oh, Nick?"

"Nick." She purses her lips. "I like Nick. Do you like Nick? He's got a great body. What does he do for a living?"

"Ah . . . aren't you married?"

Michelle shrugs her shoulders. "Meh." She sips at her margarita.

What does "meh" mean when you ask someone if they're married? Either they are or they aren't, right?

Doug opens the screen door and brings out a huge mug filled to the brim with strawberry margarita, topped off with an umbrella straw. He sets it down in front of me, then moves to sit next to Michelle.

The evening is filled with small talk about the weather, the roads, the small town, if Mr. Peterson is going to allow another chain restaurant to build downtown. Right now the only thing we have is Denny's. The drink helps the words flow out of my mouth, and before I know it, I'm telling them things about Alex and my sister. Things I haven't even told people at work. When I get to the bottom of the margarita, I'm feeling more than woozy. I try to remember the last time I had a drink. It was with the pizza. I stop drinking and leave the last inch of slushy margarita in the mug. Michelle starts nodding off in her chair and Doug has a strange, accomplished look on his face.

"Well." I push the mug away. "I think I should get home." As I stand, I wobble a bit.

Doug stands and Michelle mumbles, "Why don't you help her, dear? She's so young and small."

Even intoxicated I can recall that those two words have never been used to describe me.

Doug holds my elbow as I descend the steps to the deck. When my feet hit the grass, I push him away.

"I'm fine." I think I slur. Jeez, I hope I didn't slur.

"It's all right. I'll help you," Doug says.

"Don't need help." I take a few steps, feeling very strange. I've never felt like this after a night of drinking. Ever. Maybe I'm getting old.

Doug steps away, raising his hands in the air, letting me wobble away.

Thankfully, I make it to my back door without falling. As I stand there twisting the door handle, I catch Doug watching me, smiling, like a super-creeper. I wonder what's up with Doug and Michelle.

And then, out of the corner of my eye, I see the flick of a white tail and hear the stomping of hooves.

Something is behind the garage, but I'm too tipsy to investigate. I'd probably fall on my face.

October 10, 2012

I wake to the sound of someone shouting a string of curse words. I cross the bed to glance out the bedroom window, where I can see directly into the Richardses' yard. Doug stands there, face red as a tomato, surrounded by deer shit.

"Holy hell," I whisper to myself with a giggle.

It doesn't look like one deer took a crap while passing by; it looks like an entire herd had a party on his deck and emptied their bowels.

I watch Doug for a few minutes as he heads to the garage and wrestles out a power washer.

The rest of the day is filled with the steady hum of the power washer's motor running, as Doug does his best to clean up the mess.

After sleeping most of the morning, I make my way to the kitchen for coffee. As I turn the corner from the living room, I notice something out of place. The saltshaker I took over next door last night is sitting by itself on the middle of the island countertop.

My heart beats hard as I run to the back door and check the locks. The dead bolt is open and only the lock on the door handle is engaged. I always lock the dead bolt. Maybe I forgot.

The hum of the power washer makes my head pound as I try to remember what exactly I did last night. I don't remember bringing the saltshaker home. I don't remember locking the door, but it's one of those things you just do.

I take a quick glance around the house and everything seems to be in its place. I can only hope that I simply forgot to lock the door, or maybe Doug or Michelle brought my saltshaker back and locked the door for me. It's creepy, thinking that someone could have been in my house while I was passed out sleeping.

I make a cup of coffee and try to forget it.

November 5, 2012

Exactly one year after writing Nick a check for ten thousand dollars, the past due notices start showing up again. I march my ass down to the gym the evening the mail arrives.

I don't know what I expect I'm going to see when I get there. It's been over a year since I've been in the place. I envision it kind of like a party: barely dressed chicks, men sporting greasy biceps and ripped tank tops, champagne, and loud music.

Walking my way across the parking lot, I prepare myself for battle. I put on a pair of jeans and a light sweater, in case I have to get in a verbal dispute and start sweating. I bet I'm going to have to unplug the blasting radio and tear Nick off some hot blonde while he leans over her and shows her how to bench-press with correct form.

When I rip open the front door, there's no music. Only the hush and swish sound of an elliptical machine in the corner. And there's not a hot blonde on the elliptical; it's a middle-aged lady wearing a shirt that says something about the Salty Scarlet Sisters. The gym still smells strongly of disinfectant and rubber, but it's much cleaner than the twenty-four hour gym I was using over the winter. I pass the front desk, which is a mess and unmanned, and make my way to the office door in the back.

Okay, this is it. I prepare myself for battle once again as I reach for the door. Nick's probably playing video games on the computer, or bending some Octagon groupie over the desk. I pause before touching the door handle. This could get awkward. Who am I kidding? It's always awkward.

Please don't be bending some Octagon groupie over the desk. Please don't be bending some Octagon groupie over the desk. Please don't be bending some Octagon groupie over the desk.

Taking a deep breath, I twist the door handle and shove the door open.

Nick is sitting there behind the desk. He looks up, a bit startled, but he's not doing any of those things I was preparing myself for. He's also not doing the things I would expect a business owner to be doing. He's not elbow deep in bank receipts and statements and pay stubs—nope. Those are textbooks and notebooks spread across his desk.

I don't even know what to say. But, "what are you doing?" is what comes out of my mouth.

"Studying." Nick blinks at me.

"Studying?" I ask.

The stack of bills in my hand feels like it weighs a thousand pounds.

"I can't fight forever," Nick says as he stands. He seems huge in this office, filling up the space so that there's barely any room to breathe.

"Fight?" I ask, at a loss for words.

"Yeah, that's what I do for money. Remember? The Strangler. It's not like the memberships bring in enough to pay the bills here. Alex could have told you tha—" Nick stops himself from revealing more.

Yeah, he could have, but he didn't. There's a lot he didn't tell me. Like that he was independently wealthy. Like I probably could have sat around our little house and ate bonbons, or I could have bought a freaking mansion and tanned my pale ass in the sun all day and bought a billion books on the Internet.

Whatever.

"Money . . ." I've suddenly lost the ability to form a coherent sentence.

"Yeah, money. It's what makes the world go round."

Nick gives me this look, like *what the hell are you doing here?* I hold up the thousand-pound stack of overdue bills.

"Money also pays bills," I say, feeling like a dick.

"Sure does." His face drops when he sees the bills.

"What's going on, Nick? I mean, fighting, school, running this place—when do you sleep? This isn't healthy."

He stands and walks close to me, the heat pouring off of him, making me sweat. I wish I had worn a T-shirt.

"When do you sleep with all the double shifts and the running?" he asks.

I step away from him. "Don't answer a question with a question," I reply.

"Doesn't matter. I'm dropping out." The words come out in an exasperated hush, like he's giving up.

"What? Why?" I don't want him to give up.

He looks at his watch. "I have class in twenty minutes. I can't lock up and leave. I'll miss the evening rush. And I can't afford to miss the evening rush. *And* I can't afford to hire another employee. I won't be making it tonight. I only have one more absence left before I've missed too many classes to pass."

Oh no. The realization hit's me like a brick: Nick has no Ark either.

Okay, I'm part owner, so this should be easy.

I can do this.

I think I can do this.

I can do this, right?

"Why do you keep saying 'I,' Nick?" I want to scream at him, the solution is so simple. "I'm still your business partner. No matter how many times you try to buy me out. This place is still part of me. It's my last connection to . . . *him*." I pause to clear the thickness in my throat. "I'll watch the gym. You go to your class."

There is a brooding, shifting-on-his-feet, giant dude standing in front of me now, trying to determine if I'm serious.

Finally he just asks, "Seriously?"

"Yes." I wave my hand at the door. "Go."

And then he starts shoving the books from the desk into a backpack. "I'll be back before nine." He pushes his arms through the straps and pauses for just a second. "Thanks," he says as he heads toward the door, and just as he passes me, he bends and brushes a swift kiss across my cheek. My face reddens instantly and I don't turn to watch him go. Instead, my hand moves to my cheek and a feeling fills my chest. I push it away. It was nothing, just a kiss on the cheek like he would give his sister. I wonder if he has a sister? I had a sister, but we never shared hugs or kisses on the cheek like normal siblings do. Maybe we should have. Maybe then Nick's cheek-kiss wouldn't have felt so strange.

~

I thought working in the emergency room was hectic. That is nothing compared to the evening rush at Sullivan's Gym. People want water and towels, they want to sign up for memberships, they want information on what muscles to work, what to bench press, how long to do their cardio for, and how to use the saunas. They want to know when we're getting a pool or how to add a family member to their membership. They let me know the cooler is out of drinks, and we're out of towels, and the disinfectant spray bottles are empty. Then the kids show up for jujitsu class, but Nick isn't here to teach it, so I wind up apologizing to a bunch of angry parents. And then there's this old, overweight man, and I'm watching him get all red in the face on the elliptical, waiting for him to clutch his chest and fall over from a heart attack. I pick up the phone and make sure I hear a dial tone, just in case I need to call 911. It's good the phone works, but the rest of this place . . . it is so disorganized.

Since I'm part business owner, I do something about it. I start at the front desk, rearranging, cleaning, making notes, and labeling folders. By the time the last person leaves, I have a completely organized front desk. There are fresh sign-in sheets, newly formatted with the date, member number, time signed in, and time signed out. I've noticed a few times that people signed in without writing their member number down. I get the feeling we have a few squatters using the gym. I get on the computer and research a card machine and barcode scanning equipment. I order it all and have it express shipped directly to the gym. Just as I'm printing the receipt, the front door jingles and Nick walks in.

"Hey," I say.

"Hey," he replies, his voice sounding a bit tired. He walks around the side of the greeter desk and his face drops.

"What?" I ask innocently.

"What did you do?" Nick drops his bag with a thud on the floor.

"I organized. This place was such a mess."

I'm smiling, but he's on the verge of freaking out. Nick starts frantically flipping through the labeled folders and notes, moving the stapler and the phone back to their previous positions.

"I liked it the way it was. Why did you do this? I didn't ask you to do this. You were just supposed to watch the place, not change it all around."

I step away from him, my heart sinking. "I was just trying to help."

"Well you're not helping. This isn't helping!" His voice seems to waver between frustration and panic.

"Fine." I walk to the office quickly and get my bag. "Fine. Forget I offered," I say as I pass him.

As my hands press against the door, Nick says, "Wait."

I turn, so ready to leave that it's hard to stop the momentum of my body from pushing the door open. Nick's hands are resting on the desk, his shoulders slumped, his head down, and his thick, blond hair almost covering his eyes.

"I know you're trying to help, but what do you know about running a business? You're a nurse," he says, his voice low.

Jerk-Nick is back. I want to throw something at him, but there's nothing close enough to me.

"I know nothing about running a business," I reply. "But I know something about organization. It doesn't take a genius to recognize this place is a mess. No wonder you can't pay the bills. You probably can't find half of them. So you're fucking welcome."

I start to leave, but Nick marches around the desk just as quickly as that day I first saw him fight in the ring, and he reaches out a hand to stop me. "I just . . . I—" he starts but never finishes.

"Spit it out."

"I just wasn't expecting this. It's just been me. Alex used to do all of this stuff, and with him gone, it just got . . . out of control." He stands up straight, and I am still amazed at how he fills a room with his presence. "I guess what I'm trying to say is thank you."

"You're welcome." I take this moment to tell him that I ordered the membership card equipment.

"I can't afford that. I don't need it," he says.

So then I show him the sign-in sheets and ask for his list of current members. His face turns a bit red when he can't produce one.

"Do you even know who has a membership?" I ask.

Nick moves his arm to scratch the back of his neck. "Well, yeah, I mean I have the list of credit cards I bill each month and . . ."

"And what?"

He shakes his head. "I don't have time for this." He lifts his backpack like he's going somewhere.

"Who pays in cash or check?" I ask him. He heads for his office and I follow. "Who pays, Nick?"

Nick searches his drawers and pulls out a yellow notepad with what looks like chicken scratch all over it. He holds it out to me.

"What's this?" I ask.

"My records." Nick crosses his arms. Now he's back to looking all stoic again. I try to remember the image of him sleeping on the park bench next to me; he looked less like a jerk then.

"I've seen doctors with better handwriting. How can you even read this? Don't you have computer files? There's a computer at the front desk but there's nothing on it. I looked while you were gone."

Nick pulls a slim laptop out of his backpack and sets it on the desk.

"You must know how to use that if you're in school. Why don't you keep digital records?" I ask.

"I just don't have time. People pay me when they pay me. I use the money I win from the fights and I pay the bills when I can." Nick gives me a sheepish look. He's obviously not proud of how he's been running things, but it seems without Alex in his life, he has been falling apart just like me.

"Where did Alex keep everything?" I ask, my voice low. I don't like saying his name because every time I do, I remember how much I miss him.

Nick raises his shoulders and motions to the desk. "I don't know. He sat at this desk every day, but I can't find anything. I don't know how he organized it. Nothing. There's nothing here." Nick slams a fist down on the desk so hard, I'm surprised it doesn't break. He's fuming and I'm afraid I might be his next Octagon brawl.

I back away.

"Don't worry about it. I'll look later and check the house," I say just before hauling ass out of there.

~

As soon as I step off of my porch, I notice Nick is there, leaning up against a tall oak tree in my front yard, dressed in running shorts and sneakers. I glance at him and, remembering his freak-out session at the gym, I take off running before he has a chance to say a word to me.

Nick's footsteps are behind me.

"I'm sorry about earlier," he says as he moves next to me.

"It's not a problem."

Nick runs faster, which isn't hard for him since his legs are about a foot longer than mine. He pulls in front of me and starts jogging backward.

"It's a problem." His blue eyes are locked on my face. "I'm sorry."

I should just take the apology. I get the feeling Nick "The Strangler" Stacks apologizes to no one.

"Okay." I let myself look at him for just a second.

"Just okay?"

"What more do you want me to say about it? I tried to help. You freaked out. You apologized. I accepted. What else is there to say?"

Nick doesn't reply. He just moves to the side, slows, and turns so he's running next to me. I don't worry about his lack of response. I know he's a man of few words and many moods.

When we get to the park, I slow and jog in a tight circle.

"When do you have class again?" I ask.

"Tomorrow. Why?"

"Well, I was thinking I could watch the gym for you while you finish up the semester."

He seems to mull it over for a bit.

"It's okay if you don't want me to," I say. "I can't promise I won't rearrange things again."

"No. I think that's a good idea."

"Okay." I smile a little. I don't know why, but I can't seem to control the tugging coming from the corner of my lips.

"I mean," Nick starts, "you are part owner. We are business partners."

"Yeah." I start making my way home. "We are."

"So I guess you should spend some time there. Especially since you won't let me buy you out."

Ouch. That burns.

"I mean ... there are no other employees, so having someone else around would be good."

As I near my house, I slow to catch my breath so I can say, "I have something for you."

"Okay." He seems a bit leery regarding my offer. I haven't even told him what I have, but I'm sure he's used to getting naked bodies thrown at his feet and offers for steamy one night stands, so this should be easy.

"You want to come in, or you want to wait out here?" I ask.

"I'll wait out here."

It shouldn't bother me, the fact that he won't step foot in my house. I try to tell myself it's not because he can't stand being in an enclosed space with me, but that maybe being in my house reminds him too much of Alex.

I take the laptop off my dining room table and bring it out to Nick. It took a few hours of searching but I found Alex's computer in his nightstand. After digging through the files, I found the ones for the gym. Thankfully, there were no passwords on anything and there were already spreadsheets made out and half-filled in from just before he died. Alex was like that: super organized with the business. I guess that's what an Ivy League business school education will get you.

Nick gives me a look as I descend the porch with the laptop in my hand. "Here." I hold the computer out to him. "I found the gym laptop. All of Alex's files are there for the budgets and stuff."

Nick reaches out and takes the computer from me. "You sure you want me to have this?"

"Well, you can start filling stuff in now, and next time I'm at the gym I'll work on it. Then it can stay in the office."

"That sounds like a good idea."

"Sure. Oh, there's one more thing."

"Yeah?" Nick looks down at the black laptop in his hands.

"Alex's truck. It has the gym logo painted all over it." I point toward the closed garage. "It's been stored in there since . . . since, you know. It's too big for me to drive. I didn't know if maybe you wanted it."

Nick looks at the closed garage door, his forehead wrinkled in thought. "I already have a truck."

"Sure. Well maybe if you hire another employee," I offer.

"I'll keep that in mind."

The awkward silence is back.

I suck in a breath and say, "Okay good night see you tomorrow." The words come out as one long string.

Nick just nods, and then I turn and run into the house.

Watching through the window, I see Nick walk away from my house slowly with the computer in his hands, holding it like I placed a baby there for him to take care of.

I rearrange my work schedule so I can watch the gym while Nick finishes up the semester. We do this for weeks. Cynthia smiles a bit too widely when I tell her why I need to change my days and drop a few of the extra shifts I had picked up weeks ago.

"It's not what you think," I warn her.

"Uh-huh." Her fingers tap away on her keyboard while she makes the changes.

"It's just business. I'm part owner. Did I ever tell you that?"

"Never." The printer makes strange noises as it gets ready to spit out my schedule.

"Alex's best friend is the other part owner. He fights too," I add, and I'm not sure why.

"Oh yeah." Cynthia's eyebrow tips up and she looks genuinely interested. "What's his name?"

"Nick Stacks."

"The Strangler?"

"Yeeeeaaaah." I draw it out. "How do you know his ring name?"

"I have a second cousin; he did MMA for a while. I went to a few events."

"You did?"

"Yeah." She spins in her chair and reaches for the piece of paper on the printer, with my new schedule on it. "You should go. They're entertaining."

I shake my head. "I tried once. It was too violent. I couldn't sit through it."

"Oh." Cynthia crosses her hands on her desk and eyeballs me. "Is he your Ark?"

"No," I answer quickly. "He's just . . . a friend. Maybe . . . Probably not even that. I don't know. I'm just helping him out so he can finish up his degree."

"Sure," she replies, the corner of her mouth tipping up.

"It's nothing," I assure her.

~

That night, after our usual run, we stop in front of my house. I'm out of breath, but Nick looks barely winded. I guess that's the benefit of having been in shape your entire life, and being so tall, and so muscular.

"I have a fight on Friday." He gives me a sheepish, crooked smile, which makes me wonder if he's nervous.

He's not nervous.

He can't be nervous.

Guys like Nick don't get nervous, right?

"Want to come?" Nick asks.

"I can't," I blurt out before even giving it a second thought.

His hand moves to the back of his neck.

I think he's actually nervous.

"I've been to one of your fights before. Alex took me not long after we were married," I say.

"Oh." Nick sounds surprised, like he didn't even know I was there. He probably didn't. He never looked at me once when I was with Alex. This is nothing new to me. I knew I was invisible to him and to plenty of other people.

"I'm not saying no because I don't want to support you. I'm saying no because I spend my life fixing up broken people. I can't stand the violence. Not when I have people walking into the ER who are beat to crap. I just can't watch it."

"I understand."

"If it were something else, I'd go. Like if it were downhill skiing or turtle racing, I'd be there. I just can't watch that."

"Sure." He actually sounds disappointed, and I feel a bit bad letting him down like this.

Something sparks in my head. "Hey, Nick?"

"Yeah."

"Why do they call you The Strangler?"

He smirks a little. "Peruvian necktie."

"Huh?"

"It's a move. The Peruvian necktie. Knocks them out every time."

"Oh. Sounds a bit dangerous."

Nick rocks back on the balls of his feet. His face is lit up a bit, like he's enjoying talking about fighting. "It can be, if the other guy doesn't tap out. It pretty much cuts off the circulation to their—" He stops midsentence. "Sorry. You probably don't want to hear the details."

Remembering Cynthia telling me she enjoyed watching her second cousin fight, I encourage him to continue. "It's okay. Cuts off circulation?"

"To their head. So, you know, The Strangler." He makes a motion with the crook of his elbow across his neck.

"Sure. I get it." I take a deep breath. I'm sure that's what that move does: cuts off the carotid artery. Dangerous.

"Want me to show you how to do it?" He takes a step toward me, and it's a bit frightening.

"No. No." I back away. "I don't need to be strangled."

He laughs, and just as I'm admiring his smile, the sound of breaking glass causes us both to turn toward my neighbor's house.

"Holy crap." Nick steps closer to me. I can feel the heat radiating off him.

When my eyes focus in the shadows, I see a deer up on its hind legs, hooves on the side of the deck to support itself, jabbing at the camera with its antlers. It's deliberately damaging the camera.

"Oh my God" I blurt out.

And, as if the deer hears us, it turns to face us with a piece of plastic hanging off the tip of one of its antlers. Tilting its head to the side, it makes a grunting sound, much softer than the way the deer did when that cameraman surprised me at Alex's roadside vigil. Then the buck takes a few steps to the Richardses' flower bed and begins munching on the flowers.

"They are gonna be so pissed," I whisper.

"Well, hopefully they got that on video. That's definitely a deer."

"Yeah." I pause and watch as the deer consumes all ten plants in the garden bed. "Maybe you should strangle it for them."

Nick chuckles softly. The deer raises its head and ambles toward us.

"Hey, buddy." Nick holds his hand out, palm up. The deer stretches its neck and sniffs before looking at both of us.

"I think it likes you," I whisper out of the corner of my mouth.

"You have any bricks to throw at it? I'm sure you can't miss being this close," Nick jokes.

I back away. "I hate deer."

The deer snorts, obviously bored with us, then it turns and begins walking away, across the neighbor's front lawn and down the middle of the street.

"That was the strangest thing I've ever seen," I say.

For a moment I wonder, since this strange deer keeps showing up in my life, maybe Alex's soul is in that deer. Maybe he's watching us. I remember Natasha's words: *I expect his soul will return as some elegant creature.* Is an eight-point buck elegant enough for Alex's spirit? I watch the buck as it gets farther away, its strong body erect, the heavy antlers balanced on top of its head. Maybe the buck is elegant.

"Do you think . . . ?"

"What's that?" Nick asks.

"Nothing. Never mind."

"It's kind of majestic," Nick says quietly. "Even if you do want to shove a brick through its head."

Those people without an Ark, who live through what you've lived through, they simmer in bitter hatred for all the joys in life.

Is having this buck interact with us considered a joy in life? Because I have developed a bitter hatred for the deer in this town. I can't sort it out. I can't understand it. Everything in my brain is so scrambled in this second. As I watch the buck walking away and Nick gazing at it, something tightens in my chest. Whatever is happening, it's nothing I've prepared myself for. I can't deal with any of it right now.

"I have to go," I mutter quickly to Nick and run into my house. Slamming the door closed, I engage the dead bolt and slide down to the floor.

December 1, 2012

One task I despise is grocery shopping. Our local store is small and everyone in town goes there. Thankfully, it's open around the clock, so I save my shopping trips for night, when the possibility of running into someone I know is low.

When I pull into the parking lot, there's only six other cars here. Hoping that they're owners are mostly employees, I venture inside. Pulling my list out of my pocket, I grab a cart and start making my way through the aisles. The list is perfectly organized, written out in the order of how the store is laid out. This should take me ten minutes, tops. I grab my milk and yogurt; last is the coffee. I make my way down the aisle, but when I get to the shelf where my favorite brand is, it's empty. Ugh. Now I have to spend extra time deciding on an alternative. When I finally decide and set the can into my cart, I hear footsteps behind me.

"Hey." A familiar voice beckons me to turn around.

Nick's here.

I force a smile. But I don't want to smile, so I try to stop it and frown a little. What the hell is wrong with me? I don't interact with people well. It was all so easy with Alex. I hate this.

"Hey," I say and let my face do whatever it wants, which turns out to be a big, stupid smile.

Nick is wearing jeans and a T-shirt that's a little tight on him. I try not to stare but his pectorals are screaming, "Look at me!"

I try to distract myself with talking. "Midnight shopping?" I ask.

"Yeah."

The way Nick rests his arm on the shelf next to him and leans into it makes me think that maybe he's looking for a little conversation. Trying to extend the socialization of having margaritas with my neighbors a few months ago, I get a crazy idea, like maybe we could have dinner, you know, like after a run. Like normal people do.

"Do you eat . . . um . . . I mean . . ." I bite my lip and blink. Why is this so hard?

"I eat." A tiny smirk starts to form on his face.

"I mean . . . I'm trying to socialize more." Gah! I sound so stupid. Why am I bothering? Nick and I can barely stand each other's company, I think. I can't think. He confuses the shit out of me.

Nick looks in my cart. He takes note of my groceries. "Does that go well with this?" He holds up his basket, and all I see are chicken breasts and frozen mixed vegetables. The basket must weigh fifty pounds, but he lifts it in the air like it weighs nothing.

How does he survive on that?

"That's all you eat?" I ask.

"My mom keeps giving it all away to the church for potluck dinner. She keeps trying to feed me pasta every night."

"You don't like pasta?"

"I like pasta. Just can't handle it the days before a fight."

"Oh. Maybe you should lighten up and not be so hard on your mom for giving away your chicken and vegetables."

One brow lifts in jest. "*I* need to lighten up?"

"Ah . . ."

Wait. What just happened? Are we having light banter or arguing? I thought I was joking. I suck so bad at this. Did I seriously just piss him off over a grocery basket of chicken and vegetables? Maybe I can change the subject?

"Anyhoo . . . all this could make a horrifying potluck dinner." As I motion to our groceries, something shiny catches my eye in his grocery basket. It's a bag of butterscotch candies. "Sweet tooth?"

Nick looks a little embarrassed over my observation. "Oh, that's for my . . ."

Girlfriend? Mom? He doesn't answer; instead he twists and grabs a box of crackers off the shelf. "I was looking for these." He glances at his watch, and I take the hint.

"Okay, well, nice talking to you."

Not even giving him a chance to say good-bye, I walk as fast as I can to the checkout.

Holy awkward.

"Are you going to do another gym membership at that local place?" Nick asks me as we jog.

He hasn't said a word about my almost-but-not-quite asking if we should eat a meal together at the grocery store the other day. Thank God. Although, I'm not sure why it bothers me; he asked me to breakfast that one morning, and I told him no. It probably bothers me because I acted like an idiot.

"I don't know." I wipe the sweat off my forehead. Somehow, even though it's barely forty degrees I'm still sweating like a pig at the county fair. "It was really bright there and didn't smell very sanitary."

"What about our gym?" Nick asks.

Our gym. I've never heard him refer to it as our gym, even though we are partners.

"I'll give you a discount on the membership."

I bet he says that to all the girls. Since I'm too winded to roll my eyes, I can only get out "I'm sure you will."

"Actually, when you're part owner, the membership is free."

"Must be nice."

"I'm serious, Morgan."

I think about it for a few seconds. "I don't know."

"Why?"

"I just . . . I just don't like the bright lights and the noise. I run at night because of the dark and the peace. If I go back to another gym, I'm going to lose that."

"Hm." Nick is quiet for a few minutes. "So are you just going to keep running outside all winter? What happens when the snow is up to your hips?"

"I'm not sure."

We run in silence for a few moments.

"Are you taking classes over winter break and for the spring semester?" I ask.

Why can we talk now, but the grocery store was such a disaster? It seems I can't hold a conversation with Nick unless half of my brain is distracted and I'm not looking directly at him.

"Yeah. Then I'll be done," Nick answers.

"So you want to keep doing this?"

"What?"

"Me, watching the gym while you finish up your classes."

"Yeah. That would be great."

"Okay."

As we come to a stop in front of my house, motion detecting floodlights illuminate the neighbor's entire side yard and the side of my house.

"Holy crap." Nick shields his face, and in the brightness, I notice he has a black eye.

"Why do you have a black eye?"

Nick turns his back to the light. "Had an event two days ago." He rubs his hand over his face, flinching when his fingers meet the area around his left eye.

"How are you out running right now? Shouldn't you be home recovering?"

"Nah." He waves a hand, dismissing my concern. "I have to keep in shape. Cardio is the most important part of MMA. I won't grapple for a week, but I have to keep up the cardio."

"Oh." The nurse in me wonders if he has any other injuries.

"So, your neighbors, they weren't happy about that buck trashing their camera and flowers."

I nod. "I think this is a bit overkill though."

"Yeah. Me too."

Just then a strange sound fills the night, a digging and pawing, the sounds of rocks and dirt hitting wood. The floodlight dims, and then with a loud *crack*, the light goes out.

"What the hell?" I say.

As our eyes adjust to the darkness, I make out the form of that buck, standing in the Richardses' yard, kicking up dirt and grass and rocks with its hind legs.

"Nice," Nick whispers.

"This is not good."

The deer unearths the freshly planted evergreen shrubs. It doesn't even eat them; it just digs them up and leaves them lying in the yard, like it's pissed at Doug for not replanting the petunias. Then the deer lets out a huff and gallops off down the road until it's out of sight.

"It's kind of beautiful," Nick says. "Even if it is a bit destructive."

December 14, 2012

Nick walks into Sullivan's Gym.

"Hey." He looks around the open space. "Is everyone gone?"

"Yeah." I finish what I'm doing on the computer.

Nick flips the "Open" sign to "Closed" and clicks the lock. "Don't go, okay?" he says as he heads for the back office.

"Sure." With a few keystrokes I save the monthly budget for the gym. The lights go out, then the television in the corner of the room, which is usually off, lights up.

"Is it on?" Nick shouts from the back office.

Turning, I get a glimpse of him half-dressed. He's changing out of jeans into gym shorts and a T-shirt. Even in the shadows of the dark gym, I can tell his body is amazing. Like Alex's was. But Nick has more bulk and he's taller. My face heats with embarrassment. I look away. Catching Alex was a "never-event," meaning it's never going to happen again. A girl like me doesn't get that lucky twice.

"Is it on?" he asks again.

I snap out of it. "Is what on?"

"The television."

"Yeah."

The door creaks and his shadow passes through the gym. "Come here." The sound of the treadmills powering up fills the room.

"Where's here?"

"Over here." Nick clicks on a small light in the corner of the room. He's bent down, pressing buttons on a remote. As I cross the gym, the television flickers to the news. I cringe. I hate the news. Nick pushes more buttons on the remote, and the screen darkens before it flickers again, and the image of a glowing crescent moon and twinkling stars appear on the screen.

Nick stands and rests his arm on the treadmill closest to him. "I can't make winter go away, but you don't have to spend your entire winter running at that other gym."

What is this thing that Nick just did for me? And what do I say in response? I can't think of a thing, so I blame my lack of words on my poor upbringing and just smile at him.

Good thing I came in sneakers, yoga pants, and a sweat jacket. You know, working at the gym, you need to look the part for customers to trust you.

I move to get on one of the treadmills and adjust the speed to the pace of a fast walk.

"Better than the other place?" Nick asks as he turns the volume up on the television, the sounds of crickets and peepers and dull-hooting owls fill the room.

"I think so."

"How's the view?" he asks.

I focus on the television screen. "Perfect."

"If you get bored I can change it. I got this DVD. Watch." He presses a button, and different images appear: beaches, forests, and volcanoes, each image with its own sounds. The last is a crackling fireplace.

"Is that a Yule log?" I ask.

"I think so." He changes it back to the night sky. "Better?"

I laugh lightly. "Better."

My mother invited me to dinner for Valentine's Day. I meet her and my father at one of those hibachi steak house restaurants. The place is packed. They should have known better than to invite me to this. I don't like crowds or strangers.

When I find my parents, I notice there is a guy in a suit standing next to them. It's as I'm giving my father a hug that I notice the guy isn't just standing next to them, he's standing with them.

When Dad pulls away, my mother introduces us.

"Morgan, this is Bill Winslow."

"Hi, Morgan." Bill gives me a hearty handshake. He's short, mostly round and his hair is a fluffy cloud of brown curls. "You're just as lovely as your mother said you'd be."

I give my father a look. He shrugs with a half frown. Had I known I was getting set up, I would have put something nicer than jeans and a sweater on. Or I would have canceled.

"Well, thank you . . . um . . . Bill." I release our hands. "I had no idea you'd be here. Who are you, again?"

"Oh, dear, Bill is our neighbor's son. You know, the Winslows in the blue house. Bill is their youngest. He's a car salesman at that big place near the mall."

"A car salesman?" I ask, just to be sure I heard her correctly.

"Highest seller in the county." He has this high pitched, annoying chuckle that makes everyone around us turn and look at him. "Need a car? We'll get you a car." He clucks his tongue and makes this strange motion with his hand, pointing at me when he's done. "Selling the deals."

With the realization that my mother just set me up on a blind date, with a car salesman, I cringe. Of course this is the kind of man my mother would see me with. She knew Alex was too good for me, just like I knew he was too good for me. My heart sinks.

The hostess calls our names and seats us at a long table with two other couples.

My mother makes a fuss of telling everyone where to sit. "Now you two sit together." She points to two chairs at the end of the table.

I order a stir-fry dinner and a rum and coke. The drink makes me a little less uneasy, but it's still awkward, the conversation is still forced, and I'm still hating my mother right now. As the meal winds down, I happily reach for my purse on the floor and get ready to leave.

"Well, it's late." My mother stands and pulls my father up with her, halting my escape. "You two kids stay and have a few drinks. Get to know each other."

She moves toward me and bends to hug me. "He's nice, Morgan. Give him a chance. You don't want to be alone forever," she whispers in my ear.

"Night, girlie." Dad pats my shoulder and gives me a look that says "sorry."

"Another round of drinks?" Bill asks the waitress. "Come on." He takes my hand. "We'll go sit at the bar. Get to know each other."

I pull my hand away. "I'm driving."

"A few drinks won't hurt you."

He must not know that my sister died in a drunk-driving accident. Or he does and he's just a jerk.

"You cleaned up nice since you were a kid, Morgan." Bill leans into me, and I can smell the booze on his breath. He settles a hand on my thigh, and his gaze goes straight to my boobs. "Real nice." His other hand moves to my cheek, brushing my hair away from my neck, and he leans in.

I stop him with a hand on his chest. He feels like a marshmallow under his shirt. "No."

"No what?" Bill asks, his voice a bit teasing.

"No . . . just no."

"Come on, baby. Your mom said it's been years. You don't want to be alone forever. If it's about money, I've got money. I know women worry about money." He pulls three twenty-dollar bills out of his wallet and tucks them into the pocket of my jeans. "I read those dirty books everyone's been reading. I'll sweep you off your feet just like the guy in those books. I've got lots of money. I'll give you a ride in my BMW. Will that make it better?" He stands and presses his hips against my leg. I can feel the bulge behind his slacks, and cringe. I am so not into this

135

guy, or anything about him. And why is he all over me like I'm some easy date? Like I can't do better than him? Like I have no other option but him. Well, that's probably what my mother told him. Maybe that's what's giving him his confidence right now.

"I can even give it to you rough, just like all the girls like now," he adds, and I almost vomit in my mouth. Is that what girls are into now? Rough sex with rich men? Alex was never rough; he was always sweet and patient and attentive. I don't want rough sex with Bill. I don't want *any* sex with Bill. I have to get out of here.

I stand and give him a little shove away from me. "I'm sorry . . . um . . . Bill." I think his name is Bill. I don't really care what his name is. "I'm just not ready for that kind of a relationship. I have to go."

His face changes in an instant and he stands up. I'm not super short, but I was always shorter than Tori, and Bill seems so much taller now, I have to tip my head up to see his face. "I don't get shot down."

"Excuse me?" A few people at the bar next to us turn to look.

"I can make you happy, Morgan." Bill bends and his breath is in my ear, his hand moves to my hip, and my stomach churns sickly. "So sit down and finish your drink," he demands. "It cost me twelve dollars." My face inflames as his hand presses on my hip, trying to force me to sit. "This is what the women like now, right? Someone to tell them what to do, put a collar around their neck, and treat them like crap. If that's what you want, I'll do it." He pushes my hip harder.

I guess I'm sending him the wrong signals, so I pick up the drink and throw it in his face. "Actually, Bill, I don't like that and I'm not thirsty." I reach into my pocket and throw his money back at him. "And I don't need your money."

I run out of the restaurant, faster than I've ever run anywhere. When I get to my car, I don't even turn around; I just drive as fast as I can out of there. As I'm leaving the parking lot, I notice a red BMW with the license plate "STD#1." I'm sure it stands for his slogan "Selling the deals," but the humor in the fact that he has a license plate with "STD" on it doesn't escape me.

Dodged a bullet on that one. What a douche. Bill the car salesman. I could kill my mother right now.

For some reason, I'm a bit too afraid to go home. After all, I did throw my drink on Bill, and I wouldn't put it past my mother to tell him where I live. So I drive to the nearest safe place, the gym.

"Hey," Nick sounds distracted when I pop my head into the back office. "What's up?"

"Nothing." I look around the nearly empty gym and feel a bit out of sorts. "Do you mind if I walk on the treadmill and have a customer water?" I need to sober up. I don't admit that last bit to him.

He waves his hand. "Go for it."

I grab a bottle of water from the fridge, kick off my boots, and set the treadmill to a slow walk. I'm sure I look ridiculous, wearing jeans and a sweater and walking the treadmill in my socks. But since I'm the only person working out at the gym on Valentine's Day, I don't really care.

After an hour, Nick leaves the office and starts shutting the place down. I turn off the treadmill and put my boots back on.

"You don't have to stop," Nick says as he packs up his backpack. He's distracted. I think I remember him mentioning something about having a project due tomorrow.

"I should get going. I'm ready for this evening to be over."

"Bad night?" Nick asks.

"You could say that."

"What happened?"

"My mom set me up on a blind date with some douche-hole."

Nick chuckles.

"It wasn't funny. It was actually kind of awful."

"Anyone good?" he asks.

"Bill Winslow. He's some car salesman at the mall." I make my way to the front door of the gym to leave.

"Need a car? We'll get you a car." Nick mimics the slogan that Bill said so proudly to me.

"I don't need a car."

"Well—"

"I threw my drink on him." It comes out like a confession. I regret it, since I don't usually do those things. But part of me feels like he deserved it.

"Awesome."

I reach for the door. "Don't ever buy a car from him or I'll hate you forever."

Nick looks up from the front desk just as I'm opening the door. "Morgan."

I pause. "Yeah."

"I'm sorry you had a crappy night." He gives me that crooked smile and for an instant I wonder what Valentine's Day dinner with Nick would have been like. Since everything always seems a bit awkward and tense between us, I'm sure I'd end up dead after mocking his chicken and vegetables again. Peruvian necktie dead.

"Me too, *Strangler.*"

Nick just gives me a quick smirk and continues on with packing up his bag. He probably has a hot date. A guy like him definitely has a hot date tonight. He's going to do all those things that Bill was whispering in my ear to some young hot college girl. Good for him. Good for her. I leave before something stupid comes out of my mouth.

You don't want to be alone forever.

No, I don't, but I'm not ready to fill Alex's memory with a loser like Bill. I go home, alone. Just like Bill the car salesman said I would. And on my way there I stop at a convenience store and buy three books to read tonight. I may not have much of a life, but I can read about someone else's perfect life.

When I step up onto the porch to let myself in, I notice something near my feet. Bending, I find a single red rose and inspecting it, I notice the bottom of the stem isn't cut cleanly, like it would be from the florist. Instead, there are long shredded plant fibers, like someone ripped or gnawed it off of the rose bush. Feeling like I'm being watched, I turn to see the eight-point buck standing under the streetlight. It seems to watch me for a moment before turning and walking down the middle of the road, away from me.

March 4, 2013

Nick starts pulling out thick mats and laying them on the floor in the middle of the gym.

"What are you doing?" I ask.

He looks at his watch. "We have practice in ten minutes."

"Practice?"

"Yeah." He grunts as he moves a heavy mat into place. "MMA fight club. Every Monday."

"Oh." I slow the treadmill, wondering if they ever talk about fight club. This is the first I've heard of it. "Should I go?"

"No, you're fine." He begins moving another mat. "It's just . . ." He drops the mat and starts adjusting it. "You're not usually here on Monday."

I'm not. Usually I'm working, but tonight I got canceled. "I can go." I push the power button and turn off the treadmill.

"No, you don't have to go." He goes to get another mat and turns half of the lights off so the gym is still lit up but not as bright. Then he sets the radio on some heavy metal music. "Just pretend we're not here. It's fine. Really."

"You sure? Because I know the first rule of Fight Club. I watched that movie."

"It's fine. Stay." He pulls his shirt off and I look away.

I will not stare at his half-naked body. I will not stare at his half-naked body. I will not stare—*Oh, but I want to.*

"You should come on Wednesday nights. We have yoga night then," Nick says as he kicks the mats into place.

"Yuppies." I focus on the treadmill, setting a program for my run.

Nick lets out a light laugh. "It builds balance. There's nothing you want more than core strength and balance when the other guy is punching you in the face. Yoga is perfect for that."

"Makes sense." *Don't stare!* I scold myself. I grab my phone out of my bag and put the earbuds in my ears before getting back onto the treadmill and starting it up.

Halfway through my run, people start filing into the gym. And they're not just any people; they're giant men with bulging muscles, thick necks and biceps, and midsections wrapped in tense tissue. I can hear Nick talking to them over the music in my ears. His deep voice is excited through all the high-fives and arm slaps. I count twelve guys of varying ages. They're all talking about an event on the first of April. I guess he has a fight.

I try to avert my eyes as they begin their workout. It starts with cardio warm-up, and as the men jump, the entire gym shudders under their weight. Then they start grappling. They break up into pairs. Nick shows them a move and then they all practice it as he weaves between the guys, bending to show them how to improve or patting a shoulder to indicate a good job.

I try not to stare, but it's so hard.

When they're done with the grappling, they all stand on the outer edges of the mat and take turns fighting. Most of them are too tall for me to see what's going on in the middle. Part of me is glad I can't see. Each time I remember Alex taking me to that fight, I get a sick feeling in the bottom of my stomach.

As I cool down, my run becoming a walk, they're still at it. It's when I stop the treadmill and bend to get my bag that a few of them turn around and glance at me. Not knowing what else to do, I give them a nod and walk away, grabbing one of the flyers off the front desk as I pass. I saw them on my way in, advertising the fight for the first of April.

A tiny voice inside my head is telling me to go, even though the voice in my heart is telling me to stay away.

Just as I reach the door, I hear Nick's voice. "Hey!" I turn around and see him jogging across the gym toward me. I shove the flyer in my pocket. Thank heavens he put his shirt back on. "You're just going to leave without saying good-bye?"

"Oh, well . . ." I can't remember the last time he cared if I said hello or good-bye to him. "I didn't want to interrupt your practice."

"It's no big deal." He smiles as sweat drips down the side of his face and soaks his shirt.

"Okay, well, good-bye."

He winks. "Bye, Morgan. You should come back next week."

"Um . . ." I have no idea how to interpret the wink. "I don't know." I lean around him and see all the guys watching us. Suddenly, I have an intense need to get out of there. "Good-bye. See you later." I turn and rush out the door.

As I walk across the parking lot, I hear the gym erupt into man noises: heckling and shouts and profanity. I take a quick glance back to see Nick getting a punch on the shoulder and a hard shove, and the guys are laughing. I have no idea what's going on in there. It's like the place turned into a zoo. Seems I left just in time.

I get in my car and head home.

April 1, 2013

Doug and Michelle put their patio furniture out today. They also have two flats of petunias ready to go into the ground. I think they're just begging that deer to come back this year. The sight of the petunias reminds me of the Richardses' suggestion to plant some flowers in my yard, so I head to Poughkeepsie—to the closest home improvement store—in search of something to make my house look a little more to my neighbors' standards. Usually, I try to avoid shopping during the day, but since it's another town over, the chance of running into someone I know is low.

I park at the edge of the lot and enjoy the smell of spring as I walk across the pavement. The home and garden section catches my eye. There are flats of flowers in full bloom and hanging baskets that are overflowing and colorful. I veer toward them like a bee. I have never been a gardening person, but after choosing four hanging baskets and a watering can, and picking out a small flowering shrub for the front walkway, I'm starting to think that I might like gardening.

As I make my way to the checkout, I come across a display with a bunch of those yard trinkets. Gnomes and creatures holding welcome signs. Birdbaths and plastic flowers with solar lights inside of them. I figure what the heck and grab a handful of the plastic flowers. On the bottom of the display are a bunch of figurines with red clearance tags stuck to them. One is a small deer with its nose touching a purple flower that's painted on the base of the figurine. I hate deer. But this little figurine looks so sweet and innocent. Maybe if I put it out front, the buck won't eat my flowers when it comes back. I take the deer figurine and put it in my cart.

~

Done with the yard work, I shower and get dressed. Afterward, I dig through my gym bag until I find the flyer for Nick's fight tonight. My heart thunders a little in my chest. I tell myself it's nerves and do my best to get over it.

When I get in my car, I program the GPS to the location of the event, and while I'm driving, I argue with myself about turning around and going home and forgetting this stupid thing I'm doing. What am I doing? Sneaking off to one of Nick's fights after I've told everyone I can't stand to watch it. What does that make me? A liar. A jerk. I wish I could turn around and go home, but the curiosity is overbearing and wins out. No one will see me. No one will know. It will be my little secret.

My little secret, my little secret, my little secret, is my mantra as I drive.

The parking lot is packed, and I am transported back to the night Alex brought me to a fight and I freaked out. Right now I don't have the support of Alex; I only have myself. I did plenty alone before Alex, and the few short years I had with him weren't enough to make me forget the feeling of being on my own. It's just that "lack of loneliness" feels so good.

I sit in my car and watch the people as they wander into the arena. The marquee in front says "Nick 'The Strangler' Stacks vs. Josh 'The Wasp' Bledsoe."

These MMA fighters have strange names.

Women walk into the building, wearing tiny dresses and skintight leggings. I look down at my own outfit: jeans and a black top with a khaki jacket. I don't look like those other girls and I feel horribly underdressed. Oh well. I don't want to be noticed, and if there's one thing I'm good at, it's being invisible.

I get out of my car and head for the front doors. The guy at the ticket counter barely looks at me when I pay for a seat. When he's done handing me my ticket stub and a pamphlet and a few other things, he beckons the people behind me forward, effectively dismissing me. I walk in to the packed vestibule and make my way for the doors to the arena. It smells like cheap perfume, blood, and sweat. Not a good combination. My stomach rolls. I keep walking.

Last time, I had front row seats; this time, I chose the back row. If I need to make a quick escape, it will be easy, and I'm less noticeable hiding in the shadows.

I take a seat on the end, and the rest of the row remains empty as everyone crams to the front of the arena. I remember this electric buzzing in the air. Dull rock music plays, and there are lights pointed on the Octagon ring that's set up in the center of the arena.

I wait in the shadows, checking my watch every five minutes, anxious for this to start. Unease ripples in my gut as I try to forget my reaction to seeing my first fight. I look through the papers that the ticket guy handed to me. There's a pamphlet, my ticket stub, and two small trading cards, one for each of the fighters. One has a picture of Nick with that stoic expression I see on his face so much. It's not inviting or friendly in the least bit. He's wearing a pair of black shorts with red piping that looks like blood. I flip the card over, and it's filled with his stats and info. It's impressive to see how many fights he's won. I flip back to the front and focus on the eight-pack of abs he's flexing for the camera, and the bulging muscles in his arms and shoulders. I bet chicks pass these around and hide them in their purses and underwear drawers.

The lights dim, the crowd roars, and the spotlights shine on opposite corners of the arena. I look back and forth until I recognize Nick heading for the ring.

He moves between a walk and a skip, palming his hands with the fingerless MMA gloves I've seen before. His eyes scan the crowd for a minute and I freeze, afraid that he might see me. Why am I afraid? I shouldn't be afraid. But then, I pretty much feel like a stalker, since he invited me to a fight and I blew him off, and now, here I am, hiding in the shadows, watching him like a voyeur.

As Nick makes it closer to the Octagon, something I've never seen starts to happen to him. He wiggles his shoulders, shakes his arms, and seems to loosen every muscle in his body. Then he smiles widely, making kissing lips to the girls in the front row, and they go wild. Nick climbs into the ring; that's when I see the other guy. I was so focused on Nick I forgot there was another guy. Nick talks with some guy who's outside the ring; he did the same thing with Alex when Alex was the one training Nick and supporting him at his events.

The music stops and the lights center on the Octagon. The crowd is cheering. The announcer speaks into the microphone, but since I'm so far away and the arena is loud, I can barely make out what he's saying. The crowd roars when Nick holds up his hand and dulls a bit when the other guy raises his hand. A bell sounds and there is a moment where the only thing the two guys in the ring do is stare at each other. And then they're moving.

I had forgotten how fast they move; there are thrusting jabs and well-placed kicks. After only a minute the guys are on the ground. I find myself standing like the rest of the crowd. Nick and the other guy are grappling, arms and legs twist, torsos stretch, and the men move around each other in a tight ball. I can't tell who is who, but I can tell that the guy on top moves so his butt is in the air. Then he looks like he's sitting on the other guy's head. He presses his foot on the bottom man's back, preventing him from moving. Limbs tangle like a spider's legs. His arms are locked under the other guy's arms, then he pulls up. There's a lot of grunting from the ring and shouting from the crowd. The guy on the bottom taps out with his one free leg, smacking the mat two times. The guy on top stands, and I see it's Nick. The crowd erupts; the ref takes Nick's hand and raises it high in the air, announcing him as the winner. The entire fight was so quick I didn't have time to get upset or run out.

I stand and clap with the rest of the crowd. Nick stands in the middle of the Octagon while the door opens and a few scantily clad women bring him a belt. While they're walking toward him, Nick scans the crowd and, I swear to god, his eyes stop on my corner of the arena. I sit fast, praying the crowd will hide me. I hope he didn't see me. Wait, he can't see me. There's no way he could have seen me. He can't see this far in the dark arena, can he?

Thankful for choosing a seat in the back of the arena, I duck out, keeping my head down and practically running to my car. I think I escaped without being seen by anyone who might recognize me.

When I get home, I toss the pamphlet and trading card in my junk drawer in the kitchen. I don't want to get rid of it, but I'm not quite sure what to do with it right now. So it goes in the drawer, with my pens and sticky notes and empty Ziploc bags.

I stop myself before heading to the bedroom and think for a moment, feeling like something was missing from the front of my house. I open the door and walk down the porch steps, looking over all of my hard work from earlier today. The flowers are still there, untouched. But the deer figurine is gone.

Pesky neighbors. They probably reported it to Peterson because it didn't fall within the guidelines of how our front lawns should look. It's not like New Paltz has a homeowners association, but there are specific items we are not supposed to put on our front lawns, like bags of garbage, rusty bikes, couches, and other junk.

I'm a little peeved. It was just a figurine of a little deer. It was supposed to ward off evil spirits, I was hoping.

April 4, 2013

"Morgan." Nick calls as the door to the gym jingles.

"Yeah?" I shout from the back room. I seal up the last of the envelopes in front of me.

Nick says something to someone in the gym before his head peeks through the door.

"You aren't at the front desk," he says.

"I know. I'm here." I stack the envelopes in a neat pile.

"What's that?" Nick asks, motioning to the envelopes.

"Just some flyers for our current members to bring a friend and get their membership for half price. You know, like a friends and family deal."

"But . . ."

"What?"

"You didn't say anything to me about it."

I watch him for a moment. Even though he won the fight the other night, he still has a swollen spot under his eye and a small cut on his chin. I'm sure there's more damage. A person can't take hits like that without there being injuries.

"Do I need to say something to you about it?" I ask.

"Well, we are partners. It just seems like you do a lot of stuff without asking me or telling me about it." Nick sits at the chair in front of the desk.

I fold my hands in front of myself and ask, "So what would you like me to tell you?"

"What did you do while I was gone?"

"Well, I paid the utility bill, the quarterly taxes, billed the members for their May payments, and then I typed up these flyers for members to bring in their friends." I take a flyer off of the desk and hand it to him.

His eyes scan the page and he nods a bit, like he approves.

"Are we having a meeting or something right now?" I ask. "Is this something you covered in your business classes and you're practicing on me?"

Nick sets the flyer down on the desk. "Sure."

"Sure?"

"Yeah. We're partners here so we should have meetings and keep each other up-to-date with what we're both doing."

"I don't want any responsibilities. I'm just watching the place a few hours a week."

"You're part owner."

"Yeah, but—"

"So it's right that you act like part owner."

Crap. Is this him getting ready to ask me if he can buy my share again? I'm not sure what he's after, so I try to change the subject.

"Did you win your fight the other night?" I ask.

"You didn't know?"

I try to control my facial expressions and not give away the fact that I know because I was there. "I . . . didn't hear anything about it." I stand and reach for my bag.

Nick stands also. "I won."

"That's great. I think I'm done here, so I'll see you later."

I make my way for the door, but Nick steps right in front of me.

"Morgan," he says and moves a bit closer.

I respond, "Nick."

He glances down at my lips and I stand still, unsure of what exactly is happening right now. Nick leans forward and whispers, "Have a good night."

Dumbfounded, I walk around him and head out of the office. He was so close to me just now; I thought he was going to do something like . . . like . . . kiss me or something. He's messing with my head, and I don't appreciate it.

April 21, 2013

"Morgan." I melt a little inside when Nick says my name.

For the past few weeks, it's been getting worse and worse; he says my name, I get a little tingle. It's not good. It's actually pretty bad. I don't want to get into a situation with Nick. It seems kind of wrong, even if I want it to feel right. He confuses me and makes me act like an idiot. It will end badly, and I prefer to distance myself from those situations.

Ever since I snuck away to his fight, I can't stop thinking about him. Sometimes I pull the trading card out of my junk drawer and stare at it.

What is wrong with me?

"Morgan." Nick says my name again and a tiny bit of my sanity crumbles. He's huge and warm, pressed up against me. One hand on the swell of my hip, the other tangled in the hair at the nape of my neck.

How did we even get in this position? I forget. Oh, wait. Now I remember. We were running and I offered him a glass of water. Imagine that. Not coffee or tea or a nightcap, but water. When I turned toward him with the glass in my hand, he was *right here*, in my space, taking the glass and setting it down on the counter. And then his hands were on me.

Nick makes some noise between a sigh and a groan, I feel my knees give a bit, and then his lips are on my ear, just breathing, sending a hard shiver straight to my spine. God, I haven't felt like this since . . . since . . . Alex.

"Where did you go just now?" Nick asks.

"Nowhere. I'm here," I say.

What dude wants to hear you were just thinking of his dead best friend, when he's feeling you up in his dead best friend's house, and you're his dead best friend's wife?

And then his hands are off me, gripping the tile countertops so hard his knuckles are white. But he's still hanging over me, so close, his forehead resting on my shoulder. I don't miss the fact that he's breathing fast. I don't miss the fact that my nerve endings are on fire and he smells like musky, powerful man, igniting a fire inside me that I haven't felt since before Alex died. I try to dispel it, but I'm having a hard time.

"Sorry," he says as he pushes off the counter and backs away from me. "I shouldn't—" He doesn't finish.

Like an idiot, I stand there with my mouth hanging open, wondering where the hell that came from. That doesn't happen between people who don't really like each other. I thought we've just been tolerating each other. But, maybe that's our problem. Maybe that's why things get so awkward so often. Maybe we like each other a bit too much.

Nick picks up the glass of water and drinks it in three large gulps before handing the glass back to me.

"You work tomorrow?" he asks.

"No." It comes out as a croak, so I shake my head just to make sure he understands.

"Okay." He steps away from me, his face back to being frozen and stoic like it is so much of the time. "See you tomorrow."

Nick leaves the kitchen and I hear the front door close as he leaves my house.

I let myself slide to the floor and try to sort it all out. I can't come up with much, only that there is a problem with Nick running with me. I can't push myself over the edge and fall on my knees crying. It's been almost a year since I've had that liberty. I can't get those few minutes of release when I can let Alex go and be free. It's messing with me. Everything's clouding my head. But at least with Nick here, it's a bit better, knowing that someone else misses Alex like I do.

I stand and run to the front porch and see a shadow stretching down the street. I recognize Nick's frame in the night. I leave the house and follow him. He walks three blocks and then he takes a right, then a left before stopping in front of a small ranch. His truck is in the driveway and there's another car. A large Buick like an old lady would drive. I think I was right; he must live with his mother, like a serial killer. The Strangler.

When I get home, there's movement in the neighbors' yard. I freeze and focus in the dimness.

The buck is there, and it's eaten every single one of the Richardses' petunias that they just planted.

April 22, 2013

"I got him!" Doug shouts across our yards.

"Who?"

He runs toward me with a small monitor in his hand.

"That bastard buck. I got him on video eating all of our petunias. That asshole." He holds out the monitor and pushes a few buttons. "Here, look at this shit."

Doug holds the monitor out for me to see. Right there, clear as day, is the buck waltzing into their yard. It sniffs the flowers before turning and heading to my yard. The camera angle moves slightly, following the buck, and in the background I can see the side of my house, the kitchen window, and me standing next to the sink with Nick almost kissing me. The deer moves again, turning and devouring the petunias. It looks kind of pissed.

"That camera is pointed at my house," I say.

"It's what?" Doug scrolls his finger across the screen and stops on the frame when the buck seemed to be watching us.

"Right there. I don't want that. Ever."

Doug inspects the screen closer. "Hm. Looks like you had a man friend over."

"What the hell does that mean?"

"Nothing." Doug's face seems to inflame a bit in his cheeks.

"I wasn't recording you . . . I didn't—"

"Get it off my house," I demand.

"Okay, fine, fine. I just wanted to catch the deer."

"Well you've caught it, so now what are you going to do with it?"

Doug scratches his chin for a moment. "I'm going to kill it."

"What? How?"

"Maybe I'll shoot it."

"You can't discharge a firearm within the town limits."

"Maybe I'll poison it."

"Then it will have the shits all over your deck again."

"Hm." Doug scratches his chin. "You saw that last year?"

"Yeah." I stifle a laugh.

Doug doesn't come up with any more ideas on how to stop the buck. So I take time to tell him, again, to get rid of the camera, before I have Nick "The Strangler" Stacks talk to him about it. After paling a bit, Doug tells me he's taking it down.

And then Michelle comes running over to my yard. "Look what I found!" she shouts at us.

I lean around Doug. Michelle is holding her hand out and it's filled with something small and oval.

"What is it?" Doug asks.

"I found these in the mulch. I thought you had put out mothballs to keep the animals away from the flowers. But look." Michelle grasps one of the oval objects between her fingers and brings it to her tongue, taking a lick.

I can't hide the grossed out look on my face.

Doug makes the same face.

"Don't look at me like that, you two!" Michelle thrusts her hand forward. "They're not mothballs. They're butterscotch candies!"

I take one of the ovals from her hand, brush the dirt off of it and lick it. Yeah, it's a hard candy butterscotch.

"I thought you put out mothballs," Michelle says, confronting Doug.

"I thought *you* put out mothballs," he retorts.

"Don't you two speak to each other?" I ask.

Both of their heads turn quickly to look at me. They seem shocked and slightly appalled.

"Aren't you married?" I ask.

"Well . . . I just . . ." Doug shrugs and scratches his arm.

"We do. It's just . . . ah . . ." Michelle finds distraction in the treetops. "Is that a blue jay?" she asks.

Doug fiddles with the video monitor in his hand and mumbles, "We could use this to bird-watch."

"Yeah, we could." Michelle pulls on Doug's sleeve and they turn their backs to me, heading toward their house, talking about the birds and random things until they are out of earshot. They don't sit on their porch; their drinks sweat in the afternoon sun alone.

What the hell is wrong with those two?

May 13, 2013

The gym is turning a profit now that things are mostly organized. Sometimes I still use Alex's insurance money to buy things like new towels, business cards, bumper stickers, and T-shirts to sell. While Nick is taking his finals, I log invoices into the computer and wait for the evening rush. Now, this place is packed in the evenings with classes and members getting their prebedtime workout on. Nick found a few people to teach kickboxing and kids jujitsu classes in exchange for free memberships. I'm not sure what he did to get the rest of the people in here. Nick said he wore a Sullivan's Gym T-shirt to a few of his televised fights. I didn't think that would be enough to get people to sign up, but maybe it is.

The clock ticks closer to nine and still there's no Nick.

"Have a good night," I say with a smile to the last gym member to leave for the night.

I stand to shut down the lights then head to the front to turn the window sign to "Closed." With the lights turned down, I get a good look at the parking lot. My eyes scan it before I notice two forms in the shadows standing next to a truck. One is unmistakably Nick; the other is some lanky redhead wearing a skirt that is short enough to be considered a long shirt. My heart thunders in my chest. Nick looks toward the front windows of the gym as I turn the sign to "Closed." His lips move as his other hand settles on her hip, and she scoots closer. For a second I wonder if they're arguing, and then I see her kiss him.

Something in my chest wilts.

Moving away from the window, legs wobbling and nerves rattled, I make my way to the back office and hear a car door slam shut as I clear the threshold. I save the business files I was working on, shut down the computer, and search for my bag, suddenly fuming and heartbroken at the same time, and telling myself I have no right to be. What is wrong with me? I shouldn't be feeling like this over Nick, of all people.

The front door jingles.

"Morgan?" Nick's deep voice echoes through the empty gym.

Finding my bag, I throw it over my shoulder and make my way out of the office.

"Sorry I'm late," he says coolly as I make my way to the front door.

I don't answer him, and as I weave around the recumbent bikes to avoid him so I can get out of there, he says my name again and I ignore him.

"Hey . . ." Nick's voice falters; he must realize why I'm pissed. I feel his footsteps, vibrating the floor as he stalks after me. I pick up my pace, skipping a step. I'm almost to the door and the fresh night air. My hands hit the metal of the door just as one large hand wraps around my upper arm, jerking me to a stop. The jolt sends my bag to the floor as I turn to face him.

"What's wrong with you?" Nick looks down at me.

A million thoughts fly through my mind as I look up, but I can't verbalize one as an adequate response to him. I can never articulate much to him; usually it comes out of my mouth sounding screwed up.

"Morgan? What's up?" Nick demands.

Licking my lips and swallowing hard, I finally get out, "I wasn't offering to help you out so you could go around screwing your coeds, Nick."

His face twists in confusion and then anger. "I wasn't—"

"Whatever." I pick up my bag and turn to the door. I don't even bother telling him I bought a program that organizes the bills and purchases for the gym and found a cleaning company to come in three times a week to clean the place at a discounted rate. I want to scream at him that I've been helping him all this time, and all he's done is screw around. I want to ask if he's even been going to his classes or out on dates instead? How can he almost kiss me by my kitchen sink a few weeks ago and look at me like he wants to do it again, and then I find him saddling up to some chick in the parking lot?

As I storm out of the gym I wonder why I care. Why do I give a crap about jerkwad Nick, who's never been nice to me for longer than five minutes? I'm sure the only reason he's put up with me for this long is because he was using me to finish out the semester. Wait, that's a bit overkill; he's been nice to me for a few hours sometimes. Like when he dimmed the lights and played that night-themed DVD so I could run here during the winters. Everything feels so forced between us, unless we're running, and I hate it.

I'm not overreacting.

Maybe I'm overreacting?

Am I overreacting?

I don't make it to my car. I don't even hear his footsteps as he follows me out into the parking lot. Don't even get the chance to react before his gigantic hand wraps around my wrist and jerks me to a stop, again.

It seems The Strangler doesn't like to be walked out on.

"I wasn't doing what you think." His voice is angry.

"I don't care. I'm over it, actually." I rip my arm away from him. He reaches for me again, but I back away, my legs hitting the front bumper of my car. "Stop touching me." I slap at his hands.

"You're overreacting." He moves his hands to his sides, and I see them clench into fists.

"I don't think I am." My reply comes out a bit breathless and hitched. "I waited for you all night. The gym . . . I saw you . . ." I shake my head. Who cares about his girlfriend? "I've been doing you a favor. Watching the gym so you can finish up your degree. I have a life too. Maybe I had plans tonight."

"You didn't have plans. You never have plans."

"Maybe I did for once, jerk! But instead I get to wait around and find you canoodling in the parking lot with some hot chick. It's a bit rude."

""Ca—what?""

It's like he heard nothing I said.

"Screwing around!" I clarify for him.

"It wasn't what you think." He glances away from me and scans the parking lot.

"Then what was it?"

He shrugs his shoulders. "I'm just wrapping things up. Once I have my degree, I'm going to quit fighting. I'm just tying up loose ends right now. Then I can focus on the gym."

"It didn't look like you were wrapping things up—"

Nick moves closer to me, so fast, and presses his finger against my lips, silencing me. "You're more than mad."

I scowl at him and move my head away. God knows where his hands have been.

"You're jealous." A slow smile starts in the corner of his mouth.

"I'm not jealous. I waited . . . you . . . were . . . late."

Nick leans so close that I have to bend back, across the hood of my car, to get away from him and put my elbow down to keep myself partially upright. His left hand settles on the hood near my shoulder as I bend backward farther, trying to regain some of my personal space. One of his legs pushes between mine and I'm trapped. As my face flames, I'm thankful for the night to hide it—I don't want Nick getting the wrong idea.

His right hand moves to my neck to cup the back of my head, and his lips are on my ear as he whispers, "You are so jealous."

Tangled with him like this, I can't breathe. "Why would I be jealous?" With my free hand I push against his chest.

"Because." His nose rubs along my ear. "I think you like me."

No.

No.

No.

Yes . . . ?

No.

I don't like Nick. Girls like me don't like guys like Nick; we just tolerate each other. And it's a good thing, because guys like Nick don't like girls like me. He's just playing with me now, and I don't appreciate it. He's always messing with me, but I never know how to react to him.

"I don't like you—" I pause. "I mean . . . not like that."

"Um hm."

"We're just business partners and running partners. That's it." I clear my throat. "Please step away from me." I'm suddenly flaming hot.

"I don't think you want me to step away." His lips nibble on my neck, and I almost die right there on the hood of my car.

"I . . . I do." While my body is on fire, something else starts building inside me. A choking pressure. I push harder at his chest. "Off."

"No." He stops with the nibbling and just stands stills over me, like he can sense my near distress.

Even though he's not really touching me, it feels like there is a thousand-pound boulder on my chest.

"Two girls in one night. I bet that's normal for you, huh, Strangler? I'm not some floozy you picked up after a fight."

"It wasn't what you thought." His fingertips trail down the side of my neck, and I shiver.

This is so confusing to me right now. I remember the pepper spray in my bag. Taking my hand away from his chest, I reach into my bag and pull it out. Holding it up so he can see it, I say, "Off. Or I'll spray you."

"That's not nice."

I say nothing, but I feel my bottom lip tremble. What the hell is wrong with me?

Nick's eyes zero in on my mouth and even though it's dark out, I think he saw that. He stands up straight and pulls me to my feet. "I wasn't trying to—" he starts to say but never finishes.

I step to the side and walk away from him, rounding the side of my car and getting behind the wheel. He moves to my side of the car and stands there with his hands in his pockets, looking like I killed his puppy. I start my car and drive away without another word.

May 17, 2013

For Nick's last exam, I show up at the gym with my chest feeling tight and my head a bit off. I blame it on the high pollen count, but I still don't say one word to him when I walk in the door and walk across the gym to set my bag in the office.

"Thanks, Morgan," he says as he stands with his backpack. He waits for me to talk, but it never happens. The room is as awkward as our now silent runs have been the past few days. "I shouldn't be long."

I nod and turn my back to him.

Feeling like this is the end of my time at the gym, I start clearing up my loose ends. I set the bills to draw from a business account that's funded by Alex's insurance money. I leave Mr. Peterson's phone number and fax number on a yellow sticky note. Across the top I write, "I'll sell you my share." After closing the laptop, I stick the note on the cover, before standing and moving to the greeter desk at the front of the gym. My plan is to run out when he walks in and never speak to him again. After what happened the other night, I'm too embarrassed to look at him, let alone run a business with him.

Nick returns in record time. It makes me wonder if he even took his exam.

As I'm helping a new member sign up at the front desk, he heads for the office. I try to rush the customer along but the middle-aged guy isn't having it. For some strange reason, he's writing down the gym phone number on a piece of paper from his wallet. I slide him a business card just as a loud thud comes from the back office, followed by a string of curse words, and then the door slams hard enough to rattle the walls.

That wasn't the reaction I was expecting. I thought he'd be happy I was finally selling.

"Everything okay back there?" the guy in front of me asks.

"Chair probably fell over." I smile at him and show him where to sign the paperwork.

When I'm done charging his credit card and showing him how to use the membership scanner, at least a half an hour has gone by. Damn. I wanted to be long gone by now. Not soon enough, I tell our new member good-bye and file his paperwork.

When I'm done, I turn around and my face slams right into Nick's rock-hard chest. Startled, I stumble and trip over my own bag. Nick just watches me fall, and then I pick myself up off of the floor, looking like an idiot. How can a man so huge move so silently?

When I turn to face him, he's scowling. The yellow sticky note is in his hand.

"What the hell is this?" he asks.

"I—"

"Is this because of the other night?" He steps closer to me, invading my space. "Why now? Why after all these years and all of this?" He waves his hand around, motioning to the desk. "Why now, Morgan?"

"Because I'm ready."

"You're ready to what?"

"Let it go."

"No. This is some crap because of what happened in the parking lot."

I shake my head. "No," I tell him. "No, it's not."

"Why?" he demands.

"I'm ready . . ." My eyes scan the gym and instantly I know I'm going to miss the familiarity of it, the customers, the smell of the disinfectant, the feeling of having a tiny bit of Alex back in my life, even though he's dead.

"You're not ready," Nick says with a chuckling scoff. "You are not ready," he repeats.

"You trying to convince *me* or *you*?"

"You're not ready. You don't want to do this."

"You don't need me here anymore."

My words still him, and some chain reaction seems to be going on behind his eyes. "Foolish." He crumples the note in his hand and throws it at the greeter desk.

"You'll be fine without me. It's all set up."

Nick doesn't even respond; he just makes some noise in his throat, crosses his arms, and rubs his hand across his mouth. He's holding something in. Words and feelings, I bet. Something he's not used to.

Stepping away from him, I add, "We can still be running partners—"

"No," he spits out. "All or nothing."

You don't give someone who has no one an ultimatum like that. It isn't a threat if you're not afraid to be alone, just an annoying string of words.

"Well . . ." I give him one last look, up and down, and then I feel my face get hot. He's very nice to look at. "Good-bye, Nick. Mr. Peterson will be expecting your correspondence."

Turning, I walk out the door and leave him standing there. As I make my way to my car, I struggle with figuring out Nick's reaction to my willingness to finally sell. It seems like the logical thing to do. He doesn't need me anymore, and we were never meant to work together like this.

My mother's words echo in my head. *You don't want to be alone forever.* No, I don't. I guess it's time to move on, or at least try to.

May 20, 2013

Nick didn't follow through with his declaration of all or nothing. I can hear his footfalls as he runs behind me. He hides in the shadows, but I know he's there, about a half a block away, I think. He's probably still mad for whatever reason and just taunting me. He knows I haven't moved on. I work my overtime and run at night on my days off. I haven't met another person or gone out for dinner or even attempted to move on.

Well, there was that day last week when I finally put the battery back into my laptop and tried to turn it on. I had all the intentions of signing up for one of those Internet dating websites, but the laptop wouldn't work. I guess that's what happens when you shove it in a cupboard and leave it there for over two years. Or maybe, that's what happens when fate is screaming, "No, no, no, no!" in your face.

On second thought, I probably shouldn't do the Internet dating website. It would just make me look desperate. I'm not desperate, right? Just a bit messed up in the head because my mother never loved me, and my twin sister died, and then my husband died. I'm just screwed up a little, that's all.

Later in the day, I call my parents in an attempt to get a little closer with my mother after all of these years. When she finally calls me back, I'm sleeping between shifts. She leaves a voicemail and informs me that they are in Africa for two weeks, and then they're headed to Europe.

So much for that.

June 3, 2013

"Morgan?" Cynthia tips her head into the room where I'm sticking a patient for an IV. Frail, little old Mrs. Ross caught the stomach bug. I hold my breath, being this close to her, and pray I don't get it. I should have put on a mask.

"Yeah." After I push the catheter into a large vein, blood starts back-flowing. I smooth transparent adhesive over the insertion site and connect the fluids.

"We've got a guy in room six who's asking for you?"

Absentmindedly securing the IV and starting the fluids, I don't think much about a request. In small county hospitals like this one, we have plenty of frequent flyers, and once they know your hours, sometimes they show up and ask for a certain nurse or a doctor, hoping they'll get seen faster.

Cynthia clears her throat, and I realize I was completely ignoring her.

"I'll be right there." I start picking up my mess, peel off my gloves, and wash my hands. Moving to the mobile computer, I start documenting. "Just hang in there, Mrs. Ross," I tell her as I finish up. "The doc will be in to see you in a few minutes, and we'll get you feeling better." She nods and her husband steps into the room. "I'll be back to check on you soon."

Leaving the room, I take a left and head for room six.

"In there." Cynthia says as she points.

The door's closed, which isn't a good sign; it usually means a procedure is in progress.

"Am I taking this patient?" I ask as I rub hand sanitizer on my hands, sucking in a sharp breath as it burns a paper cut on my pinkie finger.

"Yeah."

I knock and wait to hear a response, but the only thing that greets my ears is the deep rumble of someone groaning in pain. That gets me moving. I grab gloves from the dispenser off of the wall and push the curtain back and freeze. There lies Nick, on his side, wearing just a pair of shiny shorts, shorts I last saw him wearing during a fight. Nick's not fighting right now. Nope, he's pressing a towel to his bloody nose, his cheek bone is swollen and red, and I can see deep purple bruises setting in and what looks like a painful set of broken ribs.

"Jesus, Nick." I glove up and reach for a set of towels and start running the sink water. "What the hell happened to you?" His left thigh is almost double the size of the right. "Is that broken?" I ask.

"Just a deep bruise. Other guy had a wicked leg kick. Think this is broken though." He tips his head toward his right arm resting in his lap.

I move to gather supplies. "Thought you were The Strangler? Did you forget your winning move?"

He shakes his head a little.

"You said you were going to stop."

"Had a title fight," he mumbles through the cloth that's pressed to his nose.

"What?"

"Title event. I told myself—" He groans as he shifts in the bed. "Madison Square Garden. You don't give up an invitation to that. Told myself if I lost, I'd quit."

"And?" I run a stack of washcloths through a tub of warm water.

"I lost."

"How did you get here?"

"Drove myself."

Jesus. He drove from the city to here. That's an hour's drive or more. "What the hell? You could have a concussion. And you were in the city; some of the best hospitals in the state are there."

"Too long of a wait. It was faster to drive here."

I squeeze the washcloths and consider throwing the bucket of warm water on him. "Alone. Not a smart idea."

"Alex used to drive me. This new guy . . ." Nick doesn't finish his thoughts.

I tense before handing him a washcloth. He doesn't take it. Then I remember his arm is probably broken, so I move closer to him.

"Close your eyes," I say.

Nick's left eye is so swollen, it's almost closed already. He flinches as I clean the blood from his face. He smells like sweat and blood, and with only his shorts on, I get a good glance at every muscle his body is layered with. I've never been this close to him before with him having so little clothing on. I need a distraction.

"What's your pain?" I ask.

"Bad."

"On a scale from one to ten."

He says nothing.

"Nick?" I haven't forgotten seeing him with that chick in the parking lot a few weeks ago. I know he's still angry with me over offering to sell my share of the gym, but Mr. Peterson has yet to notify me of the official buyout.

Nick's good eye flicks open. "I don't want any pain meds, if that's what you're trying to get out of me."

"Then why are you here?"

"Need my head checked out. Think I have a concussion."

"Can tell you right now that your skull is pretty thick, and I think you had brain damage long before tonight. This should be nothing." I toss the bloody washcloths in the laundry and grab an ice pack off of the supply cart.

Nick's body shudders as though he tried to laugh but then thought better of it. I haven't seen Nick smile much lately. Just a few times here and there. Usually he has that brooding look on his face that I'm sure makes the girls swoon with desire. But seeing his straight white teeth and his lip curl up, the pit of my stomach does this little fluttery thing. Thank god the door opens and the doctor walks in before I can think too hard about it. I can't be all fluttery for Nick after finally cutting my ties to the gym.

The doctor patches Nick up. After a few stitches, his arm in a sling, and ice packs all over, he's cleared to leave by morning. Just in time for my shift to end.

I stop in to check on him before I leave. *Out of courtesy*, I tell myself. It's the "nursely" thing to do. I tell all of my patients good-bye at the end of my shift, except for the ones who vomit on me.

"Can you give me a ride?" Nick asks.

"Me?"

"Some nurse named Cynthia said you could give me a ride home."

I lean my head out the door and focus on Cynthia, who's giving report at the desk. She smirks when she sees me, and moving her two index fingers in a half circle, she mouths, "Is that your Ark? He's hot."

I run my finger across my neck, indicating that the next time I see her, I'm going to kill her, possibly by decapitation.

"So?" Nick moves to get off of the bed.

"I guess."

Nick looks absolutely ridiculous in the hospital gown they gave him to wear over his shorts. I told him it's against hospital policy to let patients go home shirtless. And sitting beside him as he's half-naked for the ride home was something I had to avoid.

I trail behind him as he hobbles across the parking lot to my car.

"Where's your truck?" I ask.

"The guys came last night and brought it to my mom's house."

"They got your truck but couldn't give you a ride here?" I ask.

"Didn't want to leave it in the city. Probably would have never seen it again."

Nick looks horrible in the bright morning sun. His entire body is bruised. There are little butterfly bandage strips over most of the splits on his face near his eye and his mouth that I didn't notice before. Since his arm is in a sling, I jog around him and open the passenger-side door.

We drive silently to his house and when I pull in his driveway, he looks straight ahead and says, "I never told you where I lived."

I unclip my seatbelt. "I followed you home one night."

"Which night?"

"That night where—" I clear my throat. "I gave you a glass of water."

He starts to nod, but winces and stills his upper body. Yeah, he's in pain. I get out and open his door for him. As we make our way to the door, I with Nick's patient belongings bag and Nick with his busted self, the door opens.

"Oh, Nicky." A tiny, frail-looking woman appears at the door before we get to the front steps. "What happened? Who did this to you?"

"I had a fight, Ma." And while his words sound like he's giving her the brush-off, he doesn't move a muscle to shrug her away as she checks every single one of his bruises and cuts before he steps foot in the house.

"It's terrible, really, letting yourself get beat up like this," the little old lady mutters.

"Usually I don't," Nick says. "You know that."

Seeming to suddenly notice me, his mother smooths her hand over her blouse and smiles. "And who is this pretty young lady?"

"I'm Morgan." I introduce myself and hold my hand out to her. She takes my hand, gives it a tiny shake, and doesn't let go. She keeps my hand in hers as we follow Nick into the house, through the kitchen, and to the top of a set of stairs, where she finally releases her hold on me.

"I'm Maggie, Nicky's mother. So nice of you to help him. I always had a respect for people in the medical field. My sister was a nurse long ago."

I smile. Everyone knows someone who's a nurse, it seems.

The stairs creak and groan as Nick makes his way down.

"Oh, don't fall down the stairs, Nicky. You know you're not as young as you used to be."

"I got it, Ma. Would you quit treating me like a baby already?"

His mother leans into my shoulder and whispers, "You know these men, always acting all big and strong, but deep down they're still babies."

"They sure are." I smile at her before following Nick downstairs.

She pats my arm. "I'll let you get him settled."

As I'm walking down the stairs, all I can think is Nick's name is The Strangler, and he lives with his mother, in the basement. Total set up for a serial killer.

The large, king-size bed groans as Nick settles himself on it. I set his belongings on the leather couch near the stairs and walk toward him.

"You feeling okay?" I ask.

He sighs. "Fine."

I can tell by the look on his face and the stiff way he moves that he's not fine. Part of me wants to curl up in the big bed next to him and run my fingers through his hair and be his nurse all day long—*Stop it.* I scold myself.

There is a long moment of silence between us before he says, "The girl."

"She's pretty." I shrug. "Did you give her a free gym membership?"

"Morgan." His eyes are so deep and sad and I want to talk to him, but something is wrong with my insides. My heart is confused and angry, and I'm not sure why.

"Were you dating her?" I ask.

"Kind of. Sort of . . . not really."

That's it. How can he run with me three times a week, let me help fix the gym, have a near kissing incident at my kitchen counter, and have a fucking girlfriend on the side? Screw Nick. I'm over this.

"Hope you feel better." It comes out sounding not so nice.

I leave his room and walk up the stairs with his prescriptions in hand. The entire time I'm wondering why the heck I give a crap. We never made any promises to each other. Actually, we tried our best to avoid each other. I should have known when he tried to buy my share of the gym. It's a good thing I didn't sell; the gym would probably be gone by now with the way he was running it. At least it's back on track now, and I can walk away with a clear conscience.

Nick's mother is standing at the top of the stairs. I don't even think she's five feet tall. It makes me wonder how she gave birth to such a huge man.

"You know, my Nicky, he's got a big heart. Doesn't know what to do with it half the time." She moves her frail hand to my arm and rubs it as I clear the landing and step into the kitchen. "He thinks he knows what he's doing, but I'll tell you, pretty girl, his heart was broken a long time ago and it never healed." Her gaze moves to the basement door. "These past few months I thought he was getting better. More smiles on his face than I've seen since he was star quarterback in high school." Maggie leads me to the door, and I almost forget to hand her his prescriptions.

I would like to tell her that his new girlfriend was probably that reason for his recent mood change.

"These are for the pain." I hold out the small squares of paper. "He should really have them. Even if he says he doesn't need them."

Maggie takes the papers, offering me a sweet smile. "I'll crush them up and mix them in his applesauce. He likes it with cinnamon mixed in. That will mask the taste."

I wonder if she spoon-feeds it to him, but I don't deter her from her plan. Nick needs the pain meds, even if he thinks he doesn't.

"Thank you for taking care of him," Maggie adds.

On my way out the door, I notice a bowl of butterscotch candies. Nick's mom must have the sweet tooth. That's who he was buying the candy for that night I ran into him at the store. Maggie catches me looking at the bowl of candies and reaches for them.

"Would you like one, dear?"

"No, thanks." Alex always liked those. I still can't stand the taste of them.

Her voice increases a few notches. "Perhaps I could interest you in some chicken breast and frozen vegetables? You could take them home and save it for another night? Nicky is always bringing home this stuff. Terrible taste he has in food, really."

"Ma!" Nick shouts from downstairs. "Stop giving away my groceries!"

"Well if you would eat better, maybe you wouldn't be so grumpy," Maggie shouts over her shoulder, which is followed by a loud thud and a string of curse words coming from the basement.

"I better go, Maggie." I reach for the door.

"Take care, dear. And thank you, again, for watching over my boy."

My boy? Her son is a giant hunk of a man who seems to shrink in the presence of his tiny mother. But maybe that's what a mother's love can do to a person: make you feel small and safe. I have never felt that way in my mother's presence.

September 25, 2013

I haven't seen Nick in three months. I haven't stopped by the gym. I started running in the morning and have avoided him at all costs. It seems I'm strong enough to live through the death of my twin sister and the husband who was too good-looking for me, but for some reason, with Nick "The Strangler" Stacks, I can't deal with watching him with another girl. It's stupid really. We were business partners and running partners, and that's it. I don't know why I even had a tiny thought that it might go further.

For weeks I stare at the insurance money and the trust fund statements and consider running away, leaving on a cruise to someplace warm and new. No wonder my mother does it. It sounds amazing to just be able to drop everything and run away.

Doug and Michelle put up a new light and got rid of the camera. They also got a tiny, obnoxious dog that barks all day long. It's worse than the lawn mower running when I'm trying to sleep.

All I know is that the three-year anniversary of Alex's death is in a few days. I know I'll survive it, just like I have these past two years. I just wonder how much further it's going to break me, especially now that I no longer have Nick in my life. Last year he held me on that park bench during my breakdown. He was my Ark—crap, Nick was my Ark. And I pushed him away. Cynthia was right. Why is everyone else always so right and I'm so wrong?

September 27, 2013

Three long years. That is what I have endured. One more might be the end of me. I think this is why I'm so screwed up in the head. So for this anniversary of Alex's death, I don't run six miles and kiss the stars or throw rocks at an innocent deer. Nope. I work a double shift, during the day for a change, and when I head home, I drive right past my house and head for the bar down the street.

This has to end, I tell myself. And there is only one thing that can cure me. I'm sure of it: a public drowning. That's my plan. It's a pathetic plan, I know, but this is what it's come to. I can't take it anymore. I'm going to forget. I'm going to let him go.

The sad part is, I have to drink up the courage to forget him. I can't keep remembering it all. It would just be best if I forgot it. All of it. That's exactly what my parents told me to do when my sister died. That's what my mom said about Alex before she left for her vacation. She ran to the Bahamas on this three-year anniversary after leaving me a message, telling me that Bill the car salesman is still interested in me.

In the three months that I've avoided Nick, it's gotten worse—the strange feelings inside me. I didn't think walking away from him would matter, I was wrong. He's probably off canoodling with some sweet little coed and I have never felt so alone.

I thought walking away from him wouldn't matter. Being alone shouldn't bother me much, since I have spent so much of my life alone. But it does and I'm not sure what to think anymore. I tell myself it's a good thing. It gives me strength. I am the unwanted one, the unexpected one, and with that I have earned my strength. I swallow it down to the pit of my stomach and forget it. Tonight, I'm going to wash it all away with something strong and intoxicating. And then it will be done, over, finished, and I can finally move on.

The only bar in this little town is named Steve's. I used to come here with Alex on Friday nights to listen to the local bands. We'd drink and dance and pretend we were nothing but hillbillies or farmers or some other small-town couple out on the town, since we had a babysitter. Except we didn't have a babysitter. We didn't need a babysitter. We never got that far in our marriage. We didn't need a crappy bar like Steve's. Alex could have told me he was rich as shit and we could have afforded to go to the city, somewhere nice downtown. Heck, we could have even gone to one of those trendy bars in the suburbs if he wanted to save a few bucks.

I remember whispering in Alex's ear when I was hanging off of the crook of his arm on the dance floor, barely able to stand on my own two feet. I'd whisper, "Why don't you bring me to the city?" He'd laugh, wrap his arms around me, run his tongue across my earlobe just like I liked, and reply, "Too far. You know we'd never make it home."

Yeah, I knew we'd never make it home. We'd be lusting all over the place. He'd have to spend money on a hotel room from the trust fund I never knew about. And then, feeling guilty for the bill, I'd work a few nights of overtime to pay for it. I wish I had never worked overtime when I was married to him. Had I known our time together was going to be so short, I would have savored every second with him. I would have deserved him.

Why does it all hurt so much, after all this time, when I never thought he was meant for me in the first place? I don't know, but I do know that I'm going to drown all of those memories in front of all of those people, those townies and talkers who won't let me forget a moment of it. For everyone who *liked* and *shared* on Facebook and left heartfelt messages and casseroles on my front porch, tonight I'll face them—or at least the ones that come to the bar. Let's see if they have the balls to act like they know me or knew Alex.

Steve's looks like nothing more than a barn with a dark wooden door that has a circular window in the middle of it. As I push the heavy wooden door open, the noise inside ceases. They stare. They know me here, all of them. Even though it's been three years, a story like that, those pictures, they are imprinted on everyone's memories.

Does one of them wave or say hello? Nope. Figures.

I practically run to the bar.

"What's the strongest you've got?" I ask, making myself comfortable on a barstool.

The bartender finishes washing a glass, watching me with a skeptical eye before answering. Three years ago the bartender knew who I was, and my drink would be on the bar before I sat down. Rum and coke, with high-test coke, and none of that diet stuff.

"Evening," he says with a southern drawl. He's definitely new in town. He pauses, raises a brow, and judges me solely on the fact that I am a female, wearing a pink scrub top and makeup. "We got margaritas, martinis . . ." *Blah blah blah.* I listen while he lists off a number of girly-girl drinks.

I wait. I'm not here for girly-girl drinks. Nope, none of that is what I want. I need something strong, something that makes me cough after I swallow, something that might kill those brain cells off that are responsible for remembering. I want vapor in my nose. I want to breathe fire after I swallow. I want to exhale a strangled breath. I don't want a fucking margarita. I want gin, or vodka, or—"Bourbon," I tell the bartender.

The matching eyebrow rises. The old crabs at the end of the bar perk up. I recognize a few. My neighbor two houses down and the Sunday morning McDonald's gang: Bill, Jack, Buzz, and Mr. Peterson. Perfect, the mayor and my lawyer are here to witness this.

The bartender's staring. It's like a taunt. *Double dog dare ya.*

"Make it a double bourbon, one rock."

"One rock?"

"You know, one ice cube."

"Sure." He pulls a glass from behind the bar and starts pouring. "Trying to drown yourself?"

"Yup."

So that's exactly what I do. And, oh, the bourbon burns on its way down my throat, just like I want it to. My eyes water as I hold in a cough.

On the third drink, I hear the college kids shuffling in. They head for the pool table and the music machine. I slow down long enough to turn my head and as I do, my vision blurs. This is bad. I should have eaten something before I came here. I wanted courage. I wanted silence. I wanted *lack-of-feels*, not to vomit on myself in front of these people.

Why am I angry at them? Why am I angry at all? I don't know. I just want it to stop, all this feeling. I want it to end.

At least I vomited at home last year. I thought this year was going to be different; I didn't even eat an entire medium pizza this time. My stomach twists. Good thing I wore my scrubs. Easy cleanup, straight into the garbage.

I raise my hand to the southern-drawl bartender. "Ma'am?" he asks.

I tip my head and look down at myself. Am I really that old? I'm only, like, *twenty-six*. Feeling a dull throb in the center of my forehead, I remember my purpose here: a public drowning. Yes, a public drowning to make me forget and move on and let him go forever. I'm going to leave it all right here on this tacky bar top.

"Don't call me ma'am." I point my finger at him and wiggle it in a circle. "I'll have another."

"Double?" the bartender asks.

"Yes. Actually . . . just pour me two."

"Two doubles?"

"Yes." I pull a twenty out of my back pocket and slap it on the counter. The college students at the pool table look in my direction. Guess I slapped the bar a little harder than necessary. Oh well, that's what happens when I drink. Words spill from my mouth, and my body can't control itself.

The bartender sets two glasses in front of me. I spin my first glass, focus on the memories, and try to press it all to the back of my brain, then stare at the TV that's playing a muted CNN. Someone changes the channel to the local news, and I see my face plastered on the screen.

Crap.

I close my eyes as the conversations across the bar cease. There are words sprawled across the bottom of the TV for the hearing impaired, or for those who don't want the noise of the TV, but they're screaming in my face: *Anniversary, tragic, widowed, rescue attempt, #foreveryoung, trending.*

Shit.

Forget.

Forget.

Forget.

I want to forget.

I tip the glasses, one right after the other, cough, and exhale a straggled breath just like I wanted, just like I planned. I force that burn from the back of my eyes to the center of my chest and let the bourbon quell it.

Then *he* comes bursting through the door. Like he knew this was going to happen. Someone probably called him. I give the old dudes at the end of the bar a nice strong glare. Nosy bastards. I wish the old crabs around here would get a life and stop gossiping. I bet it was Peterson. I'd bet money it was Peterson. Heck, I'd bet the trust fund it was Peterson. Even though he's the mayor, he feels personally responsible for each soul in this tiny town. God forbid I get lost or injured on this night. I wonder if he figured out it was me throwing the bricks in the park. Maybe this is his payback to me.

Nick looms over me, all muscle and hard face and . . . God he's such an asshole. I don't know why he is, but he is, and I am still so mad at him for sticking his tongue down that redhead's throat.

"Trying to drown his memory and get yourself accosted in the process?" Nick asks.

My mind stills. Vapors gone. Fire breath gone. I am instantly sober . . . almost. And he knows it as I stare, mouth open, brow wrinkled.

Now, Nick is a dick, a jerk, a stone-faced son of a bitch. But the Nick I know, he doesn't use words like *accosted*. He's been punched in the head too many times. At least, that's what I've always thought. Listening to the word *accosted* roll off of his tongue like he was raised in New York City or Boston or some other freaking preppy place, it's sobering. Then I remember he was going to school. That's what I was helping him with before, back when we were business partners for a few short months. Maybe he finally graduated and got a new vocabulary.

"No one's going to accost me."

"It's Friday night in a college town." He gives me an agitated look. For a split second I think of how much better he looks from the last time I saw him when he was beaten to a bloody pulp and lying in an ER bed.

"They know me." I glare at Peterson. I notice the big, clunky, rotary dial phone on the counter next to him. Yeah, he definitely called Nick down here. How did I miss that? "Nothing will happen." I slur my words.

"Let's go." Nick spreads one huge arm across my back and lifts me to my feet. I'm as light as a feather. People stare. His arm drops. I'm still a widow. He's still the deceased's best friend in mourning. Three years is a long time but not long enough for people in this town not to talk.

"Let's go," Nick tells me again, but this time through gritted teeth.

Before he gets those two words out, I take one step and melt to my knees. Still drunk. Even if he did say *accosted*. Even if he did waltz in here like Prince Freaking Charming to save the day. He hauls me up with both of his hands on my arms. I hear the bartender chuckling as my head spins.

"What did you give her?" Nick asks in his Octagon voice. He doesn't use that voice much. Actually, the last time I heard it was when I left him that note. I'm sure it gets people to listen; no one wants to pick a fight with a six-foot-three, almost three-hundred pound MMA fighter. No one would dare confront The Strangler, even if he is retired.

No one but me.

"Only what she asked for," the bartender replies. "Five bourbons. Doubles."

"Fuck," Nick mutters.

Then, it's one arm under the legs, one across the back, and old men encouraging and clapping.

"Good man, Nick."

"Take her home, Nick."

"Glad to see there is one gentleman left in this town, Nick."

A few actually slap his shoulder on the way out the door.

I focus on the sound of his shoes crunching across the gravel parking lot. That's how small-town we are: doesn't matter that there's a state college up the street, they still don't pave parking lots around here.

"Why the hell did you think that was a good idea?"

"I was just . . ." My stomach rolls. "Just trying to stop it. Stop all the fluttering in my brain and move on. *It's time to move on.* That's what *everyone* tells me."

Nick says nothing. He carries me to his car, nope, truck. Big stupid truck, with big stupid wheels. He drops me to my feet and reaches for the passenger-side door. "You're not going to puke in here."

It isn't a question.

"I cannot confirm or deny the possibility of puking." I get the words out and then give myself an internal high five for not even slurring.

"Just don't do it."

He deposits me in his truck, his gleaming clean truck with leather seats and evergreen-scented rearview mirror hanging fish. He gets in the driver seat and starts the engine, stopping to look at me as he buckles.

"What were you thinking?" he asks.

"Was trying not to think." I look away, unable to control the squirm caused by his piercing gaze.

He starts driving. "When's the last time you ate?"

"When's the last time you gave a shit about me?"

"I promised him." His knuckles are white, scarred and scratched and scabbed. Fighter knuckles gripping the steering wheel. He's good and pissed; all he had to do was look at me.

I guess that's all it takes: a few years of faking it and one fallout. He only did it as a promise to Alex. Not because he cared. The truth stings just like rubbing alcohol in an open wound. Especially now that I know he did it because of some stupid man-promise.

All that time I spent helping him, running with him, sneaking off to his fight and staring at his trading card like a stupid teenager. I feel like such an idiot. Something snaps in me.

"Well that was your first mistake, Nick. Don't promise to watch over someone you absolutely hate."

He slams on the brakes and swerves the truck sideways in the empty street. I lurch forward, jerking against the seat belt.

He turns. "I don't hate you."

"Coulda—" My stomach lurches, and I fumble for the door handle. Bile rises in the back of my throat, and I can't say another word. Once I feel the cool air rush against my face, I let loose and vomit in the street.

196

A regular girl—a cute little city girl or gym babe or college chick sitting in Nick's truck all impressed with his muscles and looks and shit—they might get all embarrassed. Not me.

"You might want to get this thing washed," I warn him, wiping my face with the back of my hand and slamming the door closed. "And if you keep making that face at me, it's going to stay that way, Nicky."

Nick drives, fuming so hot his driver side window starts to fog. He pulls into the Denny's parking lot.

"I'm not hungry." I adjust my scrubs and check my front for spillage.

He pulls into a parking spot.

"You just worked a double. *Another* double. And I'm sure you didn't take a break to eat. Then you drank your weight in liquor. You're going to eat something even if I have to spoon-feed you."

He gets out, slams the driver-side door closed, and marches to the passenger side. I can tell by his stride he's good and pissed. Perfect. That will make blowing him off that much easier.

My door whips open.

"Let's go," he orders.

I wait and stare straight ahead. I'm not about to be bossed around by muscle-brain Nick.

"I've been on my own for three years. Three fucking years that nobody gave a shit about what I did, or where I went, or what I ate," I say.

Nick reaches across my hips and unclips the seat belt. "You're wrong, saying that."

"I will puke on you," I warn him.

"No you won't. You already puked all over my truck." He reaches in, pulls me out, and holds me tightly against his side so I don't fall as we walk to the front door of the restaurant.

We get seated in a corner booth.

A waitress approaches. "What can—"

Nick raises one large hand and stops her. "I'll have a coffee. Black. And she'll have a coffee. And a Grand Slam. Bacon extra crispy. Eggs scrambled. Well-done. Burned, actually. Wheat toast. And put the pancakes in a to-go box." He gives me a quick glance. "Get her a strawberry milkshake too."

I glare at him. Do my best to show him how pissed I am. How the hell does he know exactly what I order here?

Nick stares at me as we wait. I stare at the food-splatter on the wall behind his head. When the waitress delivers two steaming mugs to our table, I don't fail to notice when Nick opens two sugar packets and pours them into my coffee. Then he asks the waitress for skim milk instead of creamer. And then, fucking Nick, he pours the perfect amount of milk into my coffee and stirs it with my spoon. Tapping it twice on the side of the mug, he sets it on my napkin and continues to stare at me as we wait.

The food shows up.

Nick dismisses the waitress.

I stare at the wall.

"Eat, Morgan," Nick orders, taking sips of his coffee.

"I'm not hungry."

"Bullshit. Eat."

I move my focus to the plate. Everything's there, nice and warm, smelling delicious, just like I like it. But something's bubbling up inside me. Maybe it's the mushiness Cynthia warned me about, or the bitterness. Maybe I'm going to lose it.

"Is this how you plan to spend every anniversary of his death?" Nick asks, still sounding like a dick. He continues, "Or is there something special about the number three that's making you act like this?"

"Screw you."

He knows I don't do this. He's seen what I usually do. He's been there while I ran until I couldn't run anymore, verbally assaulted a deer, and defaced the park path. I grip the fork that's next to my plate. I think I want to stab it into his bulging bicep.

"Eat," he demands.

"No. I don't want your sympathy tonight."

He grunts. "Definitely not sympathy."

I'm fuming—fuming and drunk and sick of this shit. I just wanted it to stop. I just wanted my brain to stop all the buzzing and the thoughts and the dreams. I can't turn any of it off. I can't forget him.

Three years and every single day I remember pulling over on the side of the road, seeing all that blood streaked across the highway, pressing the heels of my palms to his chest, trying to get him to breathe, trying to get him to *live*.

Something wells up in my chest and my arms. Emotion, I guess. A strange tingling feeling that rolls straight to my fingertips, pulsing under my nails.

"Eat," he orders.

I want to say, "Screw you," but instead something finally breaks inside me. It bubbles up from the center of my gut where I've been pushing it all these years, and hot tears start sliding down my face. The dam breaks, the floodwaters rush, and without my Ark, I know I will drown, right here, in the middle of Denny's.

Nick ordered me everything I would normally order for myself. How the hell did he get to know me so well? I thought I was good at being invisible and people not noticing things about me. Maybe I'm wrong.

The tears that stream down my face are hot. Nick moves from his side of the table, slides across my bench, and crowds me. I feel like an idiot, crying in the middle of Denny's with the most eligible bachelor in New Paltz sitting next to me.

"Morgan," he says as he faces me, moving his face closer.

I take my napkin off the table and press it to my face, crying harder, trying not to make too much noise. "I can't." I push my free hand against his rock-hard chest.

"Don't." Suddenly I am lost in his upper body and arms. Tangled in him, I'm drowning. "Don't. Don't," he whispers in my ear.

"I . . . I can't let him go." Three years. It's official; he's been dead longer than we were married.

"I can't either." His voice is both deep and soft in my ear. "But we don't have to. Alex will always be with us. You don't have to let him go. You just have to let yourself go. Release it."

Now I've met deep-and-wordy Nick. I squeeze my eyes tightly and feel the napkin that's pressed against my face dampen with my tears. What guy says things like that? Guys who already know loss. But he hasn't let whatever haunts him go. That's obvious from his moods.

"It's okay." His hands move across my back, pulling me closer. "It's okay." Nick's face is no longer buried in my neck and hair. He's pulled away. I move my damp napkin, stained with tears for a man who's been dead longer than I knew him.

"It's okay," Nick repeats as his head dips, and I feel his lips against the skin of my cheek. And like when we were standing at my sink months ago, I take it a step further, because I want to, because I want to feel *something*; I want to feel him like that night he had me pressed to the hood of my car. I wasn't ready then, but I am now. I brush my lips over his, close my eyes, and let the last of the tears stream down my cheeks. My head swims from the drinks I had at the bar an hour ago. But Nick, Nick reacts as though he's been shot up with adrenaline. His hands come to both sides of my face, and he presses his lips hard to mine.

"Let's go," Nick says as he pulls away. He digs his wallet out of his back pocket and leaves way too much money on the table, before dragging me by my hand to his truck. His big, stupid truck with the passenger side coated in vomit. I feel a tiny bit bad about that. Only a tiny bit. Before I'm buckled, he's starting the engine and speeding the few short blocks to my house.

Since my car was left at Steve's Bar, Nick pulls his truck in my driveway. Before I even have my seatbelt unbuckled, he's got my door open, unlocking the seatbelt before my drunken fingers can figure out the mechanism. My exiting the truck is something between a fall and him dragging me. He pulls my keys from my scrub top, drags me to the front door, unlocks it, and continues to tow me inside. I assist him as much as I can, feeling only two bits sober since I was escorted out of the bar. Shoes are kicked off. Clothing is removed in a heated rush.

When we make it to my room, I see the bed, the bed I shared with Alex. I can't bring Nick there. Not yet. I'm not ready. I'm ready for *this*, just not *that*. I angle Nick toward the bathroom. Not my first choice, but my bed's not in there. And the toilet's close in case I need to puke again. That's so romantic. I don't think I'll need to puke again; it seems the first time emptied most of the alcohol from my stomach and sobered me up a bit.

Nick sets me on the vanity counter; the tile is cool against my bare bottom. His hands are on my legs, my calves, smoothing up over my knees and my thighs, until his thumbs settle in the hollows of my hips. I want him to move just a bit farther south. Feeling the bulge in his jeans pressing against me, I move my hands to release him, wondering how the hell I'm mostly naked and he's still got his pants on. As my fingers fumble with the button, my knuckles brush against his firm abdomen. He sucks in a quick breath and pulls away.

"Wait a sec."

Disappointment floods me. Is he changing his mind? Does he not want this as bad as I want it right now? As bad as I need it? I need him.

I wait, my butt freezing on the cool tile. After what seems like a hundred years, Nick strips off his pants and boxers and reaching into his pocket, he pulls out his wallet and a foil package.

Oh, good idea. I blink twice. I've seen Nick, but I've never seen him like this over the past few years. He is like a statue in front of me—all hard angles and planes and huge. Everywhere.

"You like what you see?" he asks, his voice gruff.

I blink again before moving my eyes slowly to his. "Um . . ." I swallow hard and feel that burning in the pit of my stomach; it's no longer grief but something else. "Yes," I say.

"Me too."

For a second I think that's a little conceited, but then I notice his fierce gaze is all over me. He moves closer, places his hands on each side of my face, and tips my head up and to the side, readying me for his lips, lips that are strong and smooth, just like his body. My head swims as he brushes one, two soft kisses across my lips, and just like his moods, they turn hard and demanding. Pressing against me, teasing my mouth open, when his tongue plunges into my mouth, I am lost. I can't even control the moan that forms in the back of my throat and escapes when his hands slide down my neck, my shoulders, my ribs, and my hips, jerking me hard against him.

"How long has it been?" he asks when he breaks the kiss.

"Long?" My head is swimming.

"Since you've done this."

I feel the tip of him pressing against me and instantly understand what he's asking. "Not since . . . Alex." I don't want to say his name, not in this moment, but there's no avoiding it. Yes, I'm pathetic; I haven't had sex since my husband died. I haven't dated. I haven't even attempted to look for someone or anyone.

"Morgan." His voice is soft, commanding.

"What?" Mine is weak and drunk.

"Stay with me."

"K."

"I'll go slow." His head dips for another kiss, and it's just as demanding as the previous one. He pulls on my hips, bringing me to the edge of the counter to meet him. His fingers move to touch me in places no man has touched me in three long years. I shudder hard and try to control myself, but it seems with this night of forgetting, I've forgotten how to control my own body. Maybe it's the bourbon. In seconds he has me ready, panting and squirming and unable to wait any longer. I wrap my legs around his waist and try to pull him closer. Nick's hands move to my hips, and he holds me still. The tip of him is right there, but I want him in me. I want to feel him. I want to feel something. *Now.*

"Slow," Nick reminds me with a sultry whisper in my ear.

"K," is all I get out because all I can do is feel him as he presses into me, stretching and filling me like I haven't felt in so long. "Oh," I moan.

Nick's firm, soft lips are back on mine, swallowing all the little sounds I make in my throat. He keeps a torturous pace, slow and grinding, and caresses every inch of me. I try to tip my hips and urge him to move faster. He stills me with his huge hands, holding me in place. I move my hands from the back of his neck, to his chest, to his back before sliding them down to his ass and gripping hard. This time Nick is the one that groans loudly into my mouth before tearing his lips off mine.

"Faster," I say, already out of breath and feverish. "Harder."

He shakes his head no.

"You won't hurt me."

This time he's the one that says "K." He pulls back, and then he thrusts in, hot and hard, jerking me against him, once, twice, and that's all it takes. He mutters something against my cheek, and I explode into a million pieces, shuddering and shaking. It continues on forever it seems, for both of us. Nick just holds me tightly to him, riding it out with his lips pressed to my neck.

"You okay?" he asks after a minute.

I nod, my cheek pressed against his hot shoulder. His body feels like I always imagined it would, a cozy fire, and for a second I think that I could stay wrapped around him for the rest of my life.

After a while, Nick untangles us from each other. He takes care of the condom, throwing it in the trash, before he turns and bends to pick up our clothes.

There is a scar stretched across his left shoulder blade that I've never noticed before.

"What happened here?" I ask, running my finger over the silvery mark on his skin.

"Car accident." He sets our clothes on the counter next to me.

"My sister died in a car accident."

Nick stops for a moment. His gaze focuses on my face.

"She was my twin. I mean . . . we looked nothing alike. I was born a day later. But, she died when we were in high school."

Why did I just say all of that? It took me months to tell Alex, and half the people I work with don't know. Or if they do, if they saw the news coverage, they haven't said anything. Maybe it's because Nick has gone through so much with me.

And then things get really strange, stranger than screwing my dead husband's best friend on the bathroom counter on the third anniversary of his death. The small bathroom turns cold and tense.

"Where are you from?" Nick asks.

"Just south of here. Newburgh."

Nick turns sickly white. "I have to go," he says as he stands and practically runs out of the bathroom with his clothes. I sit on the counter and hear the front door close and his truck start.

Since I'm ninety-five percent naked, I don't follow him. I move to take off my bra and start the shower. I wish I could say it sobered me, but the tears just come harder as I replay what just happened in my head.

I get dressed, choosing workout gear out of habit. When I remember that my car is still down at Steve's

Bar, I add a sweatshirt. I've never run half-drunk before, but the bar is only four blocks away. I should get my car and drive it home. As I tie my sneakers, I consider just leaving it there. Even though it's just a few blocks away, I shouldn't drive after having this many drinks. I learned that lesson from my sister's death.

When I open my front door, I see my car is already in the driveway. That was thoughtful; screw me, leave me, and still remember to bring my car home. I can't figure Nick out. One second he's sweet and almost caring and the next he's a complete asshat. What is wrong with him? Alex was never like this.

Movement outside causes the Richardses' floodlights to come on. Then their new dog starts yapping. When I turn, I see that eight-point buck standing there, still as a statue, looking at me. Judging me. Disliking me as much as I dislike it. I can tell by the curl in the buck's lip. Since I have no bricks to throw, I simply stare. Then the buck takes off down the street, looking like it's chasing after Nick.

October 1, 2013

I thought Nick was just a jerk, unstable, and a meathead. Now I think I'm wrong. After a few years of careful observation, I think he's hiding something. Something deep down in his soul that's never healed. Something worse than his best friend dying unexpectedly. It takes a few days for me to come to this conclusion after thinking about his quick exit the other night. Maybe I should get his mom to tell me what happened to him in high school.

Since we are like two broken puzzle pieces that fit together kind of perfectly, I'm not going to let him go. I've spent too much time on Nick just to let him run away because I asked him about a scar on his back. So he was in a car accident. People have car accidents every day. Tori died in a car accident. At least Nick lived through his. It could have been worse.

Since I've worked the past few nights, I haven't seen Nick since our bathroom counter incident. So, I'm going do something I've never done before. I take a nap after work. Then I shower. Then I get dressed in my gym clothes, choosing the smallest, tightest tank top I have—bought with the intent to wear it on those hot summer nights, but I've never had the confidence to actually wear it—and then I head straight for Sullivan's Gym. Well, I don't head straight for the gym. I practice taking off the T-shirt that's over the tank until I can do it smoothly. The marshmallow-white strip of stomach skin that's revealed concerns me. But, this is New York State; barely anyone has a tan. I try to forget about my pale skin.

When I get to the gym, it looks like I've hit the evening rush. The place is packed. I make my way inside and scan my membership card, just like a regular gym member would, then I head for the last empty treadmill. I'm halfway into my run before Nick exits the office. He scans the room, making sure everything is good, and when his eyes fall on me, I pretend I don't see him. I just wish my body would listen to me. Everything warms and tingles at the sight of him, but he seems to turn into a prickly statue. When he finally walks to the front desk, his movements are jerky and odd.

Good.

Just like I practiced in front of my mirror, I pull my T-shirt off, revealing the skintight tank. Nervousness sets in instantly, but after I see the look on Nick's face, it dissipates. I was never able to do anything like this before—run half-dressed. Things would have been jiggling and flopping all over the place, but now everything's tight and firm. This is my reward for three years of trying to mask the pain of losing Alex with running until I can't feel any longer.

The place is mostly empty when Nick finally walks over to my treadmill. I've been walking at a fast pace for over an hour, waiting for him to make some kind of move.

The door jingles as two people leave the gym.

Nick stops and crosses his arms, glaring at me.

"Can I help you?" I ask between breaths.

"Yeah. Put your ribs away, would you?"

"Well, friend, they're a little bit attached to my body, so that's kinda hard."

"Then put a friggin' shirt on already." The muscles in his shoulders bulge. I think I've been successful in getting him on edge.

"Why?" I press a button on the treadmill to stop it. "We don't have a 'no shirts, no service' policy here. It's hot."

"We don't." He rubs a hand over his mouth, clearly frustrated with me. "You're part owner; you should maintain a certain—"

"That's bull crap, Nick. You walk around here shirtless all the time."

"That's different."

"How?"

"I'm a guy."

Now he's pissing me off. "I'm going to ignore this conversation and pretend it didn't happen."

I step off of the treadmill, take long drink of water, and pick my bag up off the floor.

"I'm going to run tomorrow night," I tell him. "You want to come with me?"

"You sure you want me there?" he asks. The tone of his voice has changed, turning a bit regretful.

"Why wouldn't I?"

"Because of what I did."

"What did you do, Nick?"

"I . . ."

I step closer to him and get right in his space just like he did that day I offered him water after our run.

"I . . ." He pauses to clear his throat. "I was kind of a jerk."

"Kind of?"

His hand moves to the back of his neck, and he rubs the muscles there for a second. "Okay." He grimaces. "I was a jerk."

"Yeah. You were. And you were two minutes ago too."

"I'm sorry. It's just . . ."

"What?"

Nick shakes his head and turns away from me, glancing around the gym. It's empty now—unless he has a girl in the back waiting for him. Crap, I wonder if he has a girl in the back waiting for him.

The front door jingles and a large man walks in, followed by another, and another. Oh man, it's Monday, Fight Club night. And here I stand, trying to have a heart to heart with Nick "The Strangler."

"I should go." I reach for my bag and sling it over my shoulder.

The guys greet Nick and a few of them smile at me. I smile back and head for the door.

"Tomorrow," Nick shouts after me. "I'll be there."

I walk through the door that's being held open by a man who is even larger than Nick. Someone lets out a low whistle and I have no idea how to react, because, well, no guy has ever whistled at me. I make my way across the parking lot and head home.

October 2, 2013

The doorbell rings as I'm tying my sneakers. When I open the door, Nick is standing there.

"It's raining out," he says as he steps into the house, his blond hair damp and curling against his neck.

I look down at my half-tied shoes. "Want to run in the rain?"

"It's a cold rain," he warns me. "Like ice falling out of the sky."

"Yuck." I close the door behind him as he steps into the living room. Kicking off my sneakers, I ask, "Are you hungry? I can cook dinner."

"I ate already."

"Want a beer?" I ask.

"Sure."

I get two bottles from the fridge and hand him one.

"Is The Strangler nervous?" I ask, watching his slow movements as he twists the cap off the bottle and takes a long swallow.

"Don't call me that anymore."

"Why not?"

"Because I gave up fighting."

"Yeah, you did. But that doesn't mean you give up your nickname. It's kind of badass and it was a part of who you are."

"I've moved on."

"That fast, huh?"

He shrugs. "It's time."

"So you graduated?" I ask.

"Yup. I'm a college graduate now. All those charts and worksheets Alex made on the computer make sense to me."

"Why didn't you invite me to your graduation? I thought we were friends."

He runs a finger over the label on the beer bottle. "I don't know."

"What's wrong with you, Nick?"

"I just feel like I needed to move on from the fighting, but now I feel kinda lost."

"You're not lost."

"I think I am." He looks away from me and out the window that frames the Richardses' side yard.

"You're just . . . in between."

"Hm."

"I'll help you through this. You helped me through Alex."

"Alex," he whispers. Something cracks in Nick. Suddenly his face is pale and his eyes are red rimmed. Dudes like Nick don't cry; they punch things and make other people cry. Seeing him like this, it makes me a bit uneasy. Maybe Nick sees the concern on my face; he moves quickly, setting down the beer and wrapping his arms around me.

"I'm sorry," he whispers in my ear. "I didn't want to hurt you. I didn't mean to hurt you. Ever since I walked out of here a few days ago, I feel like I've made the biggest mistake of my life."

"Why did you walk out?" I find myself mumbling into his chest because he's holding on to me so tightly.

"I was scared." He loosens his arms, giving me room to breathe.

"Of what?"

"I don't know . . . Just *something.*"

"Use your words, Nick. Like a big boy."

"I don't do this . . . relationship thing."

Maybe he does that to the other girls, but I'm not letting him do that to me. "I get it. Normally you sack 'em and walk."

"I don't deserve it—not with the things I've done."

He looks away from me.

"What have you done?"

He is silent for a long time. He's not ready. That's fine. I can wait. But he's here when he could have just walked away.

I press Nick further. "Is this us? Are we more than business partners and more than running buddies?"

"Yes." He answers instantly. No hesitation whatsoever.

"Are you sure? Because I want to know that I can trust you. I want to know that I'm not going to find you boning some gym babe in the office on Wednesday afternoons when I'm not there."

"I would never." He pauses and seems to realize why I didn't speak to him for three weeks. "The girl, she was . . . we were just in a casual relationship. She went to a couple fights. What you saw in the parking lot, I had broken it off weeks before, and then I saw her on campus, and she followed me to the gym."

"That's bold of her."

He scratches the back of his neck. "It was nothing. It was over before anything happened between us. We just hooked up a few times. I promise."

"I believe you." I take a few long sips of my beer. Nick does the same.

"I've never done this before," he admits, just before draining the beer.

I shrug a little. I can't say I haven't. I've been in a similar relationship before. But there were things in that relationship that I never want to repeat. I drain my beer and let the slight buzz give me courage.

"Alex kept things from me," I tell Nick, moving toward him.

"I know." He reaches for me, settling his hands on my hips.

"I don't want to be in another relationship where things are kept from me."

"I'll tell you everything." Nick kisses me swiftly as he grasps the hem of my sweatshirt in his hands, tugging me closer to him. "Anything. Everything. Just ask."

"You live with your mother?"

He pulls my sweatshirt off and lifts me in his arms, and as he's walking to my bedroom, he explains, "Yes. Her name is Maggie. She was never married. She's sixty-two. Raised me by herself. She was a preschool teacher." He sets me on my feet and reaches for the waistband of my yoga pants. "I moved in with her . . . after Alex . . . I was having trouble . . ." His hands stop. I help him, pulling my pants off, before meeting his eyes.

"You're not a serial killer, are you?" I ask.

Nick's face twists with confusion. "No. Why would you ask that?"

"You're The Strangler and you live in your mom's basement."

Nick doesn't respond. I don't think he thought it was funny. Time to get him back on track. I unclip my bra and let it fall to the floor. I don't usually exude confidence, but he makes me feel confident. I only feel this way around him. I kind of like it.

Nick is back on focus. "What else do you want to know?" He presses his lips to my shoulder and hooks his fingers under the waistband of my panties.

"How old are you?"

"Twenty-seven."

"Do you have any siblings?"

"No. Only child." He shucks the panties to the floor. "What else do you want to know?" He takes a tiny step back and looks me up and down.

I'm slightly annoyed, standing here naked with him so close to the door. He can take off running like he did a few weeks ago. I might finally give up on us if he did that now.

"Why are you still dressed?" I ask.

Nick doesn't leave. Instead, he strips his clothes off faster than I've ever seen a man move. He takes me into his arms and before I get a chance to protest—not that I would—he drops us down onto the bed. A puff of air hits me in the face as we fall, and it smells just like Alex.

I panic. What if he notices I haven't changed the sheets in three years? What if he smells Alex on the bed? What if . . . what if . . . Silent tears start sliding down my face. Nick stops pressing his lips to places I enjoy. My chest stabs, my breath catches.

"Don't cry," Nick whispers, kissing the corner of my eye.

"I'm sorry." My lips tremble and I press them together to try to get them to stop.

"Do you want me to stop?"

I shake my head no. Hell no, I don't want him to stop.

"Morgan." Nick grips my jaw and forces me to look him in the eyes. His mouth opens like he's going to say something, like he wants to say something—words that are deep and meaningful, words that guys like him shouldn't know or admit to knowing. Whatever it is, he doesn't say it. Instead he presses his lips to mine in a harsh kiss.

I think I know what he's doing, as he wraps his free arm under my shoulders and pulls me tight to his body so there's not a millimeter between us: he's trying to block it all out. It works. Soon there is no bedroom, no bed, no house, and no sheets that smell like Alex. There is only Nick above me, his soft lips spreading kisses all over my body. He's a bit rough this time, a bit dominating and demanding with my body, but I don't mind. Actually, it makes me forget everything else.

This thing with Nick is different. He didn't just fall into my lap. I earned this. I want it. I fought for it. I fought for Nick. This is what it feels like to earn love. Hope blooms in my chest. I can think of nothing else but him.

October 3, 2013

I wash the bedsheets. Actually, I wash them and then I throw them in the garbage, and then I drive to the next town over and buy new bedsheets, new pillows, a new comforter, and a new mattress pad. I spend the day washing them and opening all the windows in the house. I spray the entire place with Febreze—every piece of cloth, every area rug, everything. By the time I'm done, the temperature of the house had dipped so low I can see my breath. But I've completed my task. I can no longer smell a molecule of Alex in the house. It makes me sad, but at the same time it's a bit freeing.

When I'm done making the bed, I stand there and admire my work. This bedding set is darker than the last. Dark purple and slate gray. Masculine mixed with feminine. I am interrupted by the sound of the doorbell.

I make my way to the front door. Nick is there, standing in the doorway. He has a six-pack of beer in one hand and a brown paper bag in the other, spattered with raindrops. I step back and let him in out of the cold rain. He's wearing black sweatpants and an unzipped hoodie over a T-shirt.

"What's in the bag?" I ask.

"My mom sent over lasagna. Homemade."

"You told her about me?"

"I didn't have to tell her about you. She's friends with Peterson. Plus she met you."

"Oh, yeah." I take the bag from him and head for the kitchen.

"Why is it so cold in here?"

"I was cleaning."

Nick reaches for the window over the kitchen sink and pulls it closed. "It's freezing."

I reach into the paper bag and pull out a small pan of lasagna that's still warm. Reaching for the cupboard for a set of plates, I ask, "You want some of this?"

"Sure."

Nick cracks open two beers and starts drinking out of one. I grab the other, then I plate the food and set forks out for us. We stand at the island counter. The lasagna is amazing.

"Your mom's a good cook," I say around a mouthful of food.

Nick nods as he eats. "She came straight from Italy," he says after swallowing.

"I don't remember her having an accent."

"She was a baby. My great-grandmother taught her how to cook like this."

"What does your mom think of me?"

"Don't worry about it," Nick says around a mouthful.

"I do."

"Why? Who cares what people think of you? The only thing that matters is what you think of yourself."

Although he's the one saying it, I get the feeling Nick doesn't live true to his words. He worries what others think of him. I saw it that night he turned on the show for the ladies at his fight.

"Well, anyways, it's delicious."

Nick chuckles. "Not if you're working out and trying to drop down into the middleweight division. Thanks to Mom's cooking, I never dropped below heavyweight."

"Is that bad?" I ask.

He shrugs, takes a bite of food, and swallows before speaking again. "It just meant I had to keep up the muscle 'cause I was going to fight huge guys."

"You're kinda huge." I say.

He smirks with a cocky rise of his eyebrow. "Yeah?"

"Not like that. I mean . . . you're *tall*." Well, he is huge, but damn, I need to change the subject. "So why did you stop by? I mean, the dinner is great, but you didn't call or anything."

"I tried your number. It doesn't work."

I think for a minute and remember the cell phone I used to have, but I took the battery out of it years ago and hid it all. "I have a regular house phone," I tell him.

"Do you ever answer it? I think the answering service you use is full, because when I tried calling, it went straight to voicemail, and then I couldn't even leave a message."

"It never rang." I pick up the phone on the wall and hear the dial tone. "It works."

"Let me check something." Nick stands and walks out the back door.

"So?" I ask when he returns a few minutes later.

"This is strange." Nick holds out a small piece of black plastic. "It was stuck in your phone line that connects to the house."

"Hm." I pick up the piece of plastic and roll it between my fingers. "Call my phone and see if it works now."

Nick pulls a cell phone from his pocket and calls my number. The phone on the wall rings and he hangs up.

"Hang on." I leave the kitchen and begin searching the living room for my old cell phone. I find it in the basket of hats and mittens. Making my way back to the kitchen, I push the battery in place and wait for the phone to turn on.

"I guess I can still use this as backup. I took the battery out when I started getting all the notifications from Facebook and Twitter."

"How old is that thing?" Nick asks.

"A few years."

"Is your contract still good?"

"I've paid on it. I just forgot about it. I don't talk to many people."

"What about your parents?"

"They're usually out of town. They travel a lot."

"Hm." Nick scrapes his plate clean and finishes his beer before reaching for another one.

I start cleaning up and ask Nick to grab a Ziploc bag from one of the drawers under the counter. It also happens to be the junk drawer where I throw everything I plan on dealing with later.

"Did you find one?" I ask, turning, only to find him standing there with a small card in his hand. Crap. It's the MMA fighter card I picked up at the fight I went to alone. His fight.

"Where did you get this?" Nick asks as he twists the card between his fingers.

My mouth opens, but I'm unable to form words.

"Morgan?" he asks, his voice softly demanding and the corner of his lip curling up a tiny bit.

He knows, so I spill it. "I went to one of your fights."

"I thought you couldn't stomach it?"

Shaking my head from side to side, I say, "I couldn't."

"But you went."

"Yeah."

"And you stayed."

"Yeah. But you won the fight in, like, five minutes flat."

Nick smirks. I knew he saw me in the back of the arena that night.

"I'm sorry I didn't tell you," I say.

"It's fine. I'm done with that life." Nick picks through the drawer for a moment before he pulls out a Sharpie and signs his name to the card.

He sets the card back in the drawer.

"I guess I better tell you why I'm really here," he says as he closes the drawer.

I turn the faucet off and face him.

"I need to know if you're serious about selling your share of the gym," he says.

"I haven't thought about it."

"You told me you'd sell. You left that note on my computer." Nick walks toward me, invading my personal space. "I need to know if you were serious or just mad that night."

"Why?" I ask.

"Do I need to send the lawyers a letter? Or are you keeping your share?" His hands touch my waist before moving to my hips, and he pulls me closer to him. "What do you want to do?"

"I'm not sure."

Nick's hands lower to my butt, then to the back of my thighs. He lifts me and sets me on the counter so we are eye to eye.

"Decide. Now," he demands.

I bite my lip and look into his eyes. Do I want to sever my ties with the gym? I kind of like working there a few nights a week. I like getting to know the members and working out there in the winters. I like spending the time with Nick. Am I ready to drop all of that? Where would it leave me, besides alone? I used to think that the gym was one of my last ties to Alex, but now it's an integral part of my life. Even if MMA Fight Club night is intimidating, it's still nice to be a part of it all. And I still haven't gotten to see yoga night.

We worked so hard together to get the gym running in the black. Am I ready to just give up and let it all go away?

I don't think so.

"I'm not selling," I say.

"Good." Nick kisses me and the world disappears.

When Nick leaves, I head to the kitchen, open the junk drawer, and pull out the MMA card he signed. I think it says his name—I can make out the N, but his handwriting is so terrible. I place the card in a small bag and move it to my nightstand.

October 10, 2013

"So are you going to run at our gym this winter?" Nick asks as we jog toward my house.

I shrug and say, "You know I can't speak in . . ." I take a deep breath. "Full sentences . . ." My breathing heavy. "At the end of three miles."

Nick laughs and we slow to a stop in front of my house. To my surprise, before I can answer, Nick's large hand reaches out and shoves my shoulder, hard. I trip over my own feet and fall onto the front lawn. As I turn, I see why he pushed me away. The eight-point buck is standing on the sidewalk, madder than a hornet. It snorts, and the mist coming out of its nose into the cold autumn air makes the animal look like it is some creature from hell, breathing smoke. It stomps its hooves, drops its head, and charges, running toward Nick.

I scramble away and move to my feet, watching.

Have you ever seen a grown man wrestling an eight-point buck? It's the craziest shit I've ever seen. Nick has his hands wrapped around the base of both antlers, trying to direct the buck's head away from his upper body, but the buck keeps stomping and shoving, doing its best to knock Nick over.

A car speeds down the street and squeals to a stop in front of my house. It's an old Buick, like an old lady would drive. Nick's mom and Mr. Peterson get out. They move fast for two old people, running up the driveway.

"You!" Nick's mom shouts. "Buck, young buck!" Maggie reaches in her pocket and pulls out a handful of butterscotch candies. She throws a few at the buck. "You there, bucky!"

She stops right next to the creature, and I'm afraid it's going to impale her with the way it's going after Nick, but it doesn't. Instead it stops rearing its head and stomping its feet and turns to face her. Maggie thrusts out her hand with the butterscotches, and the buck sniffs at them. She starts talking soothingly to the beast, and the buck begins eating the candies out of her palm, tipping its head to the side as though it is listening to every word that's coming out of her mouth. Maggie reaches out a small, wrinkled hand and rubs the buck's head between its antlers.

"Now, bucky, you need to go. This place is no longer for you," Maggie whispers as the buck eats the last candy in her hand.

Mr. Peterson stands protectively behind Maggie, ready to catch her if she falls. The buck snorts and shakes its head. Mr. Peterson grabs Maggie's shoulders to steady her.

"Yes," Maggie tells the buck. "She is not yours any longer."

"This is the strangest thing I've ever seen," I whisper as I turn to Nick.

He's panting and dripping in sweat, despite the cool weather, and blood is dripping down his left elbow. "Yeah, me too," he whispers back.

Maggie's soft voice interrupts us as she says, "Go, bucky. Go home."

Strangely, the buck turns and Maggie swats it on the back end just before it runs down the street, not in the direction of Nick's house, like it usually does, but in the other direction, toward the park that I run to each night.

The old people walk toward us. Mr. Peterson goes to Nick, and Maggie comes to my side.

Mr. Peterson talks in a hushed voice, with his hand on Nick's bleeding elbow, while Nick's mom wraps her frail arm around my shoulders and leads me in the opposite direction of the men.

My arms and legs are shaking, and I'm trying to process what just happened.

"The buck likes the butterscotch candies," Maggie whispers to me. "I've been hand-feeding him for years."

"You put them in the Richardses' garden bed?" I ask her. "Didn't you?"

Maggie rubs my arm, her frail fingertips feeling soothing and warm and a bit hypnotizing. "Of course it was me, sweetie."

"Why?"

She walks me farther away and continues talking so hushed, I have to focus very hard to hear her. "When your Alex died, Nick was in a bad way—worse than how he was after that car accident. He holds a lot of guilt, my Nicky does. That's why he took to the fighting. It was good for him. Better than drugs or alcohol. He's good at it and I'm proud of him. But it's hard for a mother to watch her only son suffer so much. So I begged him to move back home with me. I lied a little bit—told him I was sick." She pauses for a breath before continuing. "You'll understand one day when you have children of your own." She glances behind us and smiles. "They'll be beautiful children." Her old eyes seem to swim as she watches me for a moment. "Oh, where was I?"

"I don't understand what the deer has to do with any of this."

"Oh, that's right." Maggie pops a butterscotch in her mouth, sucking on it a few times before tucking it into her cheek. "I got Nicky to come back home. You see, it's where he belongs. Here, not three towns over getting confused with the riffraff. They weren't taking care of him after those fights. Then Nicky, he told me that your neighbors here were having a little deer trouble and he was spending so much time over here already and he's been so much happier. So I left the butterscotches. Bags of them. Loads of them. Those Richardses, they aren't the smartest bunch." Maggie scowls in the direction of my neighbors' house. "Watch out for them. I think they'll be moving soon." She continues to rub small circles over my forearm. "We have eyes around here; I always know what's going on with my son." She pinches my elbow. "Nicky still has a confession to make to you. He doesn't know it yet, but it is coming. And it's going to hurt both of you. Give him a chance, Morgan. You've helped him so much already. Let him help you. As much as you don't think you need it, you do."

Telling me I need help, I know it should piss me off, but this old lady has a soothing effect. I'm pretty sure she could tell me anything she wants right now— she could tell me I look like a sack of potatoes, and I'd just accept it. I think it's her fingertips on my arm; she's hypnotizing me or something.

Maggie turns me with the gentle guidance of her touch, leading me back to the front of my house. She says a few more things about love and marriage and true happiness, but I can barely hear her because all I can do is watch Nick as his fierce gaze holds mine. Mr. Peterson's lips are moving, and his frail old fingers are swirling a pattern over Nick's forearm. Maggie stops me a few inches in front of Nick, and the whole peculiar moment ends.

"Oh." Maggie holds up her index finger. "I almost forgot." She walks to her Buick, parked crooked in the street, and opens the rear door behind the driver's seat. When she turns and heads toward me, I notice something small and brown in her hand. She holds it out to me. "I'm guessing this is yours."

It's the deer lawn ornament that went missing.

"Where did you find this?" I ask.

"He left it at my house."

"Who?"

"The buck."

"Oh . . . thanks."

I take the deer figurine from her then bend and set it next to the walkway that leads to my porch. When I stand, Maggie pulls Nick down with her hands on his shoulders and kisses both of his cheeks. She then takes Mr. Peterson's hand, and they both head for the Buick and drive away.

I make eye contact with Nick.

"That was weird," I say.

"Yeah." Nick rubs his fingers over the bloody cut on his elbow.

"What did Mr. Peterson say to you?" I ask.

"I can't talk about it right now," Nick says. "What did my mom say to you?"

"The strangest things."

"I don't know what to think anymore," Nick says, and his voice sounds defeated.

I move to him and standing on my tiptoes, I wrap my arms around his neck and hold him tightly.

When he finally pulls away, he looks into my eyes for a moment before pressing his lips to mine. And then, there is a bright flash and a clicking sound. I think it's the Richardses' floodlight to scare away the buck, but as soon as it flashes, it's off, like a camera—except there is no one standing anywhere near us.

"Come on." I pull on Nick's hand and lead him inside with me.

I can't get Maggie's words out of my head. *Nicky still has a confession to make to you. He doesn't know it yet, but it is coming. And it's going to hurt both of you.*

"I want to know everything," I tell Nick as he closes the front door behind him. "Alex kept things from me. I never want a relationship like that again. There was so much I didn't know about him."

"I know," Nick says.

"He had a trust fund, and he left it all to me. He had all that money, and I worked all of those extra shifts when I didn't have to."

Nick nods like he already knows. "Alex came from old money."

"He never told me."

"He didn't tell many. He didn't want people to judge him based on that. He wanted to make it for himself. He had family in the city."

"I met them one night. They came to the emergency room. He has a younger brother. He left them all."

Nick nods like he knows all of this already. "Alex had all the family he wanted."

"Do you have a trust fund?"

"No. Definitely not." Nick shakes his head.

"I mean—I don't care if you do. I haven't touched the money. I couldn't care less about the money. I'd give it all back if I could. I would have given it all back to save him."

Nick winces like I stabbed him with a knife.

"I'm sorry," I say.

"Don't be. You loved him."

"I did. Even if I didn't deserve him."

"Don't say that," Nick says so low that I barely hear him.

"Why? It's the truth. I barely knew him. Married him on a whim. Guys like that, they don't fall for girls like me."

Nick takes a few quick steps toward me and grabs my arm. "It's not the truth."

"It is."

"It's not." He jerks me a bit. "That is so far from the truth."

It's going to hurt both of you.

234

I should just get this over with now and spare myself the pain. "It's the truth, Nick. I didn't deserve him. You know nothing about me," I say.

"I know enough."

I shake my head. "You don't."

Now both of his hands are on my arms, stilling me before him. "I know that Morgan Sullivan is the type of girl who doesn't know she's beautiful. I can tell by the baggy clothes she wears."

I wiggle my shoulders and try to escape, swatting my hands at him. "Stop." But he just grips me harder, so hard that I'm sure I'll have bruises when he removes his hands.

"You stop. Morgan Sullivan is up and down, hiding, always hiding, and I just want to crack that exterior and have her be real. I don't know why, but I want to push her to the edge until she shows her true self. And I think she wants me too."

"You're a dick."

"I'm not done." He kisses me fast and hard before continuing. "Morgan Sullivan is so stuck in her head all of the time that she can't even see how the world views her. The worst part, the part that I can't stand about Morgan Sullivan, is that she has no idea who she is. Or, at least, she *had* no idea who she was. I think you figured it out when you showed up at the gym half-dressed." His gaze travels up and down my body. "You found yourself. It looks good on you."

I struggle again. "That was nothing. I was just trying to make you mad or jealous or something."

Nick smirks. "It worked. You know how many guys from Fight Club asked for your number that night?"

I shake my head no.

"A lot."

Feeling the heat flush my cheeks, I look away from him.

"Now, do you want to know when I found myself?" Nick asks, his face turning serious again. "I found myself when I found Alex. Before him, I couldn't be trusted. I made bad decisions. I hurt people." He pauses and looks away from me but doesn't let go of my arms. "He helped me focus. Alex had a way of doing that. He trained me and got me my sponsorships. Did it in half the time anyone else could have."

"Why did you quit?"

"I lost two fights. My chances of making UFC title next year are shot."

"You could keep trying."

Nick pauses for a long time, his fingers finally loosening on my arms and moving to my face.

"I can take over the gym. You can do whatever it is that you need to do. I can cut my hours at the ER," I say.

"You would do that for me?"

"Yes."

"Why?" The sharp angles of Nick's face become apparent in the darkening room as he tries to figure me out.

"Because I kind of like you." I feel my tears slide between his fingers, and I ask, "Do you have some screwed up American dream that you need to prove to your mother? 'Cause I'm not sure I want to be part of it. I can't do that again. Fill a place in someone's plan."

"I have a dream. Just not one like Alex."

"What's yours?"

"To never repeat the mistakes I've make." Nick releases me and moves his hands to his shoulder, rubbing the muscle there and rolling it a few times, like there's an ache that he's working out.

"What mistakes have you made?" I ask. "They can't be that bad."

Nick says nothing. It's while he continues to rub his shoulder that I notice his elbow has started bleeding again. I reach for a paper towel and press it to Nick's elbow.

"We should get this cleaned up." I dab at the cut and try to determine how deep it is.

"It will be fine." Nick tries to pull his arm away.

I grip him harder. "No. It needs to be washed. You don't want infection to set in." I lead him over to the kitchen sink and use the sprayer to wash the cut. After pressing a clean paper towel to it, I tell Nick to hold it there while I grab bandages from the bathroom.

When I return to the kitchen, Nick is dabbing the paper towel on his elbow. I move toward him and open the pack of bandages.

"Do you think you need stitches?" I ask.

"No. I've had worse."

"Was your mother always a teacher?" I ask as I bandage his elbow.

"No. When I was a kid, she used to tell me she was a gypsy."

"And what does a gypsy do?" I ask.

Nick shrugs a little. "I think she told fortunes or something like that."

"She has a very soothing way about her."

"She always has," Nick agrees.

It seems just as my mother is a bit granola and bipolar, and Natasha believes in reincarnation and the supernatural, and Cynthia is rooted in her belief in God, Maggie is an old gypsy with the soothing ability to hypnotize. Is this what age holds for me: the inability to just be myself and live without the constraints of believing in something greater than all of us? I can't imagine having faith in something that would allow my sister and husband to leave me in such cruel ways.

"Morgan?" Nick's voice pulls me from my thoughts.

"Yeah?"

"Where did you go just now?" Nick's fingertips trail over my arm, and I am reminded of Maggie's soothing touch. Did she teach her son her tricks?

I crumple the bandage packaging in my hand and move away from him to throw it in the garbage. "I was just thinking," I say.

"I could tell. About what?"

"It just seems like everyone has faith in something. And I have faith in nothing."

"So."

"I just wonder if it makes life easier. Having faith."

Nick just watches me without saying a word.

"Do you have belief in a higher being?" I ask him.

"No."

I should have figured. Whatever tragedy is haunting Nick has probably cemented his lack of faith, just as with me.

"How about this," Nick suggests. "How about you have faith in us?" He moves toward me and pulls me into his arms. "Can you do that?"

"I think I can."

"I think I can too." His warmth envelopes me, and even while I relish it, there is a coldness in the pit of my stomach when I think of Maggie's words. Nick hasn't told me his secret.

October 17, 2013

For the past few days, Nick has been spending a lot of time at my house before and after our runs. I tell myself it's because living in his mother's basement is emasculating.

"We could just eat in," Nick says before draining the last of his beer. I told him that I would drive and he could drink his nerves away.

"You don't want to go?" I ask. He made reservations a week ago at the nicest Italian restaurant in Poughkeepsie.

"Not that." He shrugs.

"What then?"

"Your skirt's a little short."

I look down at myself. I thought I looked nice, trendy even, for the first time in my life. A few years ago I wouldn't have fit into this skirt or blouse or the knee-high boots. Nick closes the space between us. One hand moves to my waist and the other to the back of my leg, and, moving up, past my thigh, under the skirt, his fingers skim the lacy panties I put on to surprise him with later. He hasn't touched me like this since that night in my bedroom. This is good; I was planning on seducing him later. I want more than just a quickie on the bathroom counter and a tear-filled revelation on the bed I shared with Alex. I want to really feel Nick. And I think he wants the same.

I try to wiggle out of his grasp, but he pulls me tightly to him and buries his face in my neck. His lips flutter over my skin, kissing and teasing.

"No," I warn, pushing at his shoulders but getting nowhere because he's so huge, like a rock in the middle of my kitchen, wrapped around me. "You promised."

"You just look too good to take out," he whispers against my neck.

"You promised," I remind him again. "No work, no gym, no running tonight. Normal dinner, like normal people do." I worked myself up for a week for this night. I bought this outfit, put on makeup, and went to the salon to get my hair blown out. I've even been going over conversations in my head to get him to talk about what he's been hiding.

Nick's arms drop and he steps back. "Better be a fast dinner," he mumbles as he turns away from me to take care of his beer bottle.

As I'm grabbing my purse and keys, the doorbell rings.

"Expecting someone?" Nick asks.

"No. Not at all." I leave the kitchen and head for the door and recognize my father through the window. My mother is right behind him. "Hey!" I say and step back so they can come in. "I wasn't expecting you."

"Are you going out?" My mother asks, and I don't miss the hopefulness in her voice. She's afraid I'll turn into a crazy cat lady or something, working all the time and having no social life. "Or, do you have a date?" She smiles so wide I'm afraid her face might split. Her skin is tanned from another cruise, wrinkled from the sun damage and her age.

I feel my face flame. "Um. Yeah."

"Ooooh." It comes out like a long squeak as she hugs me and twists from side to side. "Tell me, who is he? Is he handsome?" This is the most excited I've seen my mother in a long time, and I wonder if she finally went to the doctor.

"Um . . ." I shoot a quick glance to my father, trying to judge his reaction. He's the most level-headed in the family. He lets a small smile slip out. "He's here." I turn. "Nick, come out here."

Nick's heavy footsteps leave the kitchen. He turns the corner into the living room and stops dead in his tracks. His face pales like the day I told him where I grew up. The tension in the room turns immeasurable, and I'm sure my house might burst apart from it.

I'm totally confused.

"You!" My mother's face turns sharp, like I've never seen before. "What are you doing here with her? Well?" She doesn't even give Nick the opportunity to answer. And I can't figure out what's going on as I look at each of them. "Did you tell her what you did?"

"Mo—" I start, but she cuts me off.

"How dare you show up here? You are the one . . ." Her entire body is trembling, and I can't really tell if it's from anger or something else. "You are the one who is responsible for the death of my daughter!"

Since I'm alive, that only leaves one other person: Tori.

Perfect Tori.

Wanted Tori.

Expected Tori.

Dead Tori.

Did Nick kill Tori?

Nick looks at me with his blue eyes, now clouded in emotion. I've seen the many faces of Nick, the many sides, but this one is new. This one is guilt and pain and—

"Is it true?" I ask, feeling my voice stutter.

"Morgan," he says, and it comes out of his mouth, like he's pleading.

Guilty, my heart says as it slams against my chest.

Now, my mom is the runner. I mean, I run, but I don't *run*. She runs away when things get bad, like when my sister died, and she ran away to Europe, and when I told her Alex died, and she ran away to Bermuda. My mom's the runner. Not me. But looking at Nick's guilty face, the red face of my mother, and my father in complete shock, I run. I run just like my mother, right out of my house.

I think I hear him speaking to them as I shove open the door, run down the steps, and take a quick left and head down the street. My insides feel like they want to explode.

Nick was there. Nick was in the accident that took my sister's life. I run harder, hating that I'm wearing dressy boots instead of my sneakers. The neighbors are going to have Mr. Peterson on the horn in about five seconds to tell him I'm running down the street dressed for dinner.

It's three miles to the park. I could run the distance in just over twenty minutes with my sneakers on, but in these boots—I'll make it in maybe thirty before my toenails fall off. Thankfully, it's dark, but that doesn't mean the gossipers of New Paltz are sleeping. A few curtains flutter. I swear I hear the phones dialing Peterson and Maggie.

I make it to the park, slowing to a walk to catch my breath. I leave the sidewalk, heading down the rock path. The night is clear, the stars glinting in the distance. Do they see me? I am one of trillions, I know, but I just want to know if Tori and Alex can see me as they shine down? It must be a no if this cruel fate has been bestowed upon me. My lack of faith is solidified once again. I can't even have faith in me and Nick. He killed Tori. All this time we've been connected by this.

I hear a strange sound nearby. There's a flock of deer. Wait, a flock? No, a herd. Who cares? I hate deer. I bend and pick up a few bricks and throw them all at the deer, screaming, "I hate you! Every single one of you stupid creatures!"

The deer just stare at the crazy chick all dressed for dinner hurling bricks at them, and the stars just glint down at the crazy chick all dressed for dinner, wondering if she is invisible to them also. I just want them to want me. I just want them to seek me out and hold me forever. I want to be the firstborn. I want to be the wanted one for once.

I turn to reach for more bricks but a large hand stops me.

"Peterson's going to be pissed if he has to send another crew out here to fix your mess." It's Nick.

I rip my hand away from him and back up. Nick looks amazing in the full-moon light in his dark T-shirt, dark jeans, and his brown sneaker-shoe things. Guys can get away with wearing footwear like that while dressing up. Chicks can't, but guys can. It's kind of bullshit, really. My feet are killing me in these boots. Of course, they're not meant for running.

"Go away." I hold my hand up with the brick, threatening to throw it at him.

"No."

Something in me cracks a tiny bit. "Please. I just want to be alone."

"You shouldn't be alone." His eyes focus on my hand. "You're not going to throw that at me."

I drop the brick in front of me and give him the strongest glare I can muster at this moment. As I'm stepping away from him, I'm wondering if he's going to trail his fingertips over my arm all soothinglike and hypnotize me like his mother did. I can't have faith in anyone. I can't trust anyone. This world is so screwed up.

"You say you fix broken people in the ER, Morgan, but you never take the time to fix yourself," Nick says as he steps toward me and I take two more steps away from him.

"What the hell! Of all the things for you to say to me in this second—"

Nick points at me. "You're just as broken as the rest of them."

That's it. I run for him, pounding my fists on his chest and trying to shove him away. "I'm not broken. You're fucking broken!" I yell at him.

I should have thought about taking on an experienced fighter; in all of one second he has my wrists secured and crossed, and then in some quick maneuver my back is pressed to his chest and I'm wrapped tight against him with his lips to my ear. "I can say that about you, because I was the same way not so long ago." I struggle against him, trying to get free, but he's too big and strong. "You're broken, Morgan."

"No."

"Yes."

"NO!"

"Yes." His hands grip my wrists tighter and jerk me a tiny bit.

I can't admit to that. I am not broken. I am the unexpected one, the unwanted one. I've survived this long on my own without the nurturing and love that everyone else gets.

I am strong.

I think I'm strong.

I'm strong, right?

"What the fuck do you care? You've never given a shit about anyone. I've known you for years and never once—" A huge sob catches in my throat because I know I'm lying. Something between us is brewing. We were about to go on a real date, and he asked me to have faith in us. I mean, how romantic is that—having a handsome man asking you to have faith in your relationship? That's all broken now. I lose. Again.

"You were in that car with Tori?" I ask.

"Yes."

"Why the hell didn't you tell me?"

"Because." I feel his shoulders slump. "I didn't know you were her sister. I mean . . . you said you were from the same place as me, but I thought there was no way you could have been related to her. It had to be just a coincidence. I didn't put it all together until I saw your mother. You look nothing alike. I don't even remember you from high school."

That's because I was invisible. I am invisible.

"I was nothing compared to her."

"Don't say that."

"You don't know, Nick. You didn't even know me then. I didn't even know *her*. We just didn't run in the same circles at school or at home. I hid in the shadows and she filled the spotlight. When I was a kid, I had hoped that maybe we would get closer as we got older. You know, when we were married with kids and stuff. But it's too late for any of that. My sister died and I never knew who she was."

"She was . . ." Nick just trails off, like he can't find the words, or maybe words couldn't describe her.

"What happened that night?" I ask.

Nick sighs. "We were all drinking. Tori got behind the wheel."

"That's not what my mother said—"

"She wasn't there." He snaps. "That scar across my shoulder? I was ejected. *I* told them I did it. I lied about driving, but it was still my fault. I didn't stop her. I didn't stop anyone. But Tori couldn't defend herself. She was dead. So I took the blame. I told them it was me driving." He pauses for a long moment. "Your mother doesn't want to believe the truth. The cops knew. They calculated my trajectory or some shit. Yeah, I said I did it. I didn't, but I didn't stop her from starting that car."

Holding on to my wrists, he untangles us and spins me to face him, my arms now secured behind my back. He must not trust me not to try and hit him again.

"For almost ten years I've punished myself for Tori's death. Every hit I took in the ring, it was for her. I moved away. Tried to start over. Met Alex and we hit it off really good. He didn't ask about my past, so I didn't have to explain it to him. When he died, I was lost. Moved in with my mother and tried to pick up the pieces." He leans closer to my face. "You saved me," Nick says. "And I'm not going to let you continue down this path alone. I'm done watching it."

"I'm fine."

He jerks me again. "You're not." His voice softens. "Every day you punish yourself for going to work that night, for believing you didn't deserve him, for thinking you're not wanted. You are wanted." His eyes search mine.

I struggle against his arms again. "You said you'd tell me everything. You lied."

"I didn't know. And you never told me the story about your sister."

"I can't do this." A stupid sob catches in the back of my throat, and I almost choke on it. "I don't know why you are with me. It doesn't make any sense at all."

He shakes his head and dips his face closer to mine. "You glow, Morgan. You shine. You twinkle.

And . . . I'm tired of holding back. I want you. More than I've ever wanted anyone else."

I stop struggling. I thought I only twinkled for Alex. He was the only one who ever noticed me.

Nicks eyes are so big and sad and hopeful at the same time. He tips his head and kisses me.

Maggie the gypsy warned me about all of this.

And then I'm crying. Nick lifts me and it's a feeling I've never felt before. My father only ever lifted Tori and tossed her up toward the clouds when we were children. I observed from my unwanted and unexpected space. When I lifted my arms for him to do it to me, my mother would pull me away and say, "You're too heavy, Morgan."

Nick lifts me as though I'm light as a feather. But he's strong—stronger than my father ever was. Through my blurred vision I catch the moon glowing over us. Maybe I had it wrong all this time. Maybe I am not one in a billion billion billion. Maybe I am one, and there is just me, and the rest is static noise. Maybe I glow as brightly as the moon and the stars, with a canary yellow aura surrounding me, and the souls of the ones I've lost have no trouble at all finding me. They send the deer to say, *I see you, right there in that park. I see you glowing so brightly, here. Meet our forest friends.*

Nick settles us onto the park bench.

"What about my parents?" I ask through a sniffle. I ran out of my house and left them there.

"They said they'd call you tomorrow. I told them everything."

"They're leaving for California tomorrow. I probably won't hear from them."

Nick shifts me so I'm straddling him. It's not a very ladylike position in this outfit, but since there isn't anyone out here but us, I don't really care. His hands move to my face, holding me in place as he looks into my eyes with that look I've seen him with before, the one where he's searching for words.

"I am broken." I finally admit.

Nick nods. "But you fixed me," he whispers.

I settle my hands on his shoulders. He feels so firm under the soft fabric. Firm and strong and *here*, *alive*.

"I have never had anyone like you in my life," he says, searching my face.

"I can't tell you the same. I had Alex."

"You took care of him. You took care of me."

I shake my head, disbelieving. But a strange thought comes to me as I feel his fingers flutter over my bare arms: maybe my faith needs to be with the living instead of letting my memories of the dead bog down my life and consume me.

Nick secures my face between his large, warm hands. "Yes, Morgan. You took care of me and now I'm going to take care of you." He pulls my face down to his and kisses me deeply. "Forever."

"You promise?" I ask.

"I promise. Forever and ever."

October 21, 2013

This time, I run to the park alone. I made a deal with Nick and brought a cell phone with me so he wouldn't worry too much. I need to do this alone.

I wait at the forest edge and, just like clockwork, the buck comes strolling out. Only this time it doesn't bother sniffing the grass or trotting around or anything. It looks right at me.

I reach for the butterscotch in my pocket and hold my hand out and say the words I've been practicing. Words that I know are crazy and may mean nothing, but I have to say them and I have to say them to *this* creature.

"Alex . . . ?" I whisper. It has to be him. "You have to let me go."

The buck's damp nose sniffs at my hand.

I wonder if that's what death and reincarnation are like, having a memory of someone you know you're connected to but unable to communicate to them. My heart breaks for the buck, for Alex, but this time it's not a fracturing break, just a small fissure that feels gigantic. I know it will lessen with time, because I have faith in Nick and that has already started fixing my brokenness.

The buck licks the butterscotch off my fingers; its tongue is moist and rough, and I look into its black, fathomless eyes before it turns and walks into the dark forest. As I watch it walk away, the heavy, haunted cloud that has consumed me since Alex died seems to lift away.

October 25, 2013

I dig through my purse until I find the business card with Natasha's e-mail address and phone number on it.

Normally I would send an e-mail, but this time I call the number. It picks up on the second ring.

"Hello?" A feminine voice answers.

"Natasha?"

"Yes."

"This is Morgan." There is a long pause. "Morgan Sullivan. Alex's wife."

"Yes," is all she says, like she doesn't know why I would call or doesn't want to talk to me. It has been over two years since I met her.

"I figured out what Alex came back as."

"Oh." Her voice seems to lighten, and in the background I hear footsteps and a door closing. "What is he?"

"He's a . . . a deer."

"Hm." She sounds like she's contemplating my words.

"An eight-point buck. For the past few years, it's been visiting my yard and the neighbors'. But it did something strange the other day."

"What was that?" Natasha sounds generally interested now.

"He attacked my friend."

"A boyfriend?"

"Well . . . kind of."

"Go on."

"A few days later, I went to this park where I always see him at night. At first I thought the deer was taunting me, because, you know, Alex died when a deer ran into his motorcycle. So I kept throwing bricks at the buck whenever I would see it. But it all kind of clicked when it tried to attack my friend."

"You mean your boyfriend. Nick, right? The fighter." How does she know him? Well, he is slightly famous.

"Yeah. Well, I went to the park a few days later, and there was the buck, standing in the moonlight, like he was waiting for me. It let me pet it, and then, I asked him to let me go. And the buck just walked away into the forest."

Natasha lets out a sigh. It sounds like one of relief. "Could you imagine being reborn into a creature that is not human but feels a draw and a love for a human? How hard it must be to communicate?"

"Do you think everyone is reincarnated?" I ask.

"Only the good ones."

"When I met you, you told me that your mother came back as a hummingbird. How long did she visit you for?"

"She still does," Natasha says with a faraway voice. "Every morning I come downstairs to find her on the windowsill, and after I look at her, she flutters away. Sometimes I put out a cup of dissolved sugar for her. I think the reincarnated, their souls crave sweet things. I think it reminds them of being human. You know, cookies and candies and things from holidays and special occasions."

And hard butterscotch candies.

"Why do you think she still visits?" I ask.

Natasha sniffs, like she's crying. "Because I can't let her go." Natasha sniffles on the other end. "She's never left because I won't let her. She remains in flux, confused, stuck, because of me, because I'm selfish." There is more sniffling, followed by the sound of a package being opened. The sounds become muffled as she must be pressing tissues to her face. "Thank you for letting Alex go."

When I get off of the phone, movement from outside the window catches my eye. I walk closer to the window and see movers loading the Richardses' belongings into a truck.

Next I call my mother. Dad said that they were on their way to Spain for three weeks, but maybe I can catch them before they board their plane.

I dial their number and the phone rings three times.

"Hello?" my mother's voice answers.

"Mom?" I say.

"Morgan, is everything okay? We're about to board our plane."

"Everything's fine." I pause, remembering the long conversation she and Dad had with Nick after the day they found him at my house. Everything was cleared up, but my mother still looks at Nick with hesitation. "Is there something you need?" she asks.

"I just wanted to say . . ." I guess when you rarely hear the words, it's hard to say them yourself. "I just wanted to say I love you." I can't remember the last time I said it to her.

"Oh." I can tell she's smiling on the other line. "I love you too, Morgan." In the background I can hear an announcement being made for their flight. "I'm so sorry, but I have to go. Our plane is boarding."

"Sure," I say.

"We'll chat when I get back. Okay?"

"Sure."

"Want to talk to your father?"

"Okay."

"Girlie?" My father's deep voice is on the other end now.

"Hey, Dad." Something has been bugging me and I need to ask him. "Did you take Mom to the doctor's?"

"Yeah. Yeah I did."

"And?"

His voice drops to a hush. "New medication. She's different now. Better."

"Good." Finally.

"Well, we have to catch our flight. Let's get together when we get back."

"Sure."

"Love you, girlie."

"Love you too."

I hang the phone up and smile. I find I've been doing that a lot lately. Smiling. I blame it on Nick.

November 1, 2013

"I want to drop my hours," I tell Cynthia.

"Oh?" Her eyebrows rise in surprise.

"To just one day a week."

"That's all?"

"Yes."

"When do you want to start this one-day-a-week gig?"

"As soon as possible."

"Um hm." Cynthia scrolls her computer mouse, clicking on a file before typing. "Would this have anything to do with that big, burly guy that dragged himself in here so you could patch up all of his wounds?"

I can barely control my smile. "Maybe."

"Knew it." Cynthia types on the computer before printing something out. "I see your Ark saved you from the floodwaters."

I tip my head and think about that for a bit. "I think we saved each other."

"Did you see today's paper?" Cynthia asks.

"No." I shake my head. "I don't read the papers or watch the news anymore."

"Well. I think you should see this." She takes the newly printed schedule from her printer, picks up a folded newspaper, and hands them both to me. "Maybe you should read that someplace more private."

"Okay."

"It's fine." Cynthia smiles.

"It is?" She knows what I went through with the social media outlets and the reporters after Alex died.

"I think so. See you next week, Morgan."

I leave her office and make my way out of the hospital. My shoes squeak on the heavily polished hospital flooring. As I walk away from the manager's office, I wonder if I will miss working here full-time. But, seeing Nick in his truck through the glass door entrance to the building, waiting for me in the parking lot, I get the sense that I won't.

I open the paper and search the front page. To the left there is a tiny blurb: "Multimillionaire's Widow Finds Love after Heartbreak, turn to page three."

With my heart beating wildly in my chest, remembering all the media attention after Tori's and Alex's deaths, I stop before opening the doors to the outside and turn to page three. And then I stand there and read the article.

Multimillionaire's Widow
Finds Love after Heartbreak

By MICHELLE TROUTMAN
NOVEMBER 1, 2013

Reclusive Sullivan's Enterprises heir, Alex Sullivan, lost his life in a tragic motorcycle accident three years ago and left behind his young wife, Morgan Sullivan, formerly Morgan Taylor. Mr. Sullivan also left behind one of the largest estates to date. Overflowing from the spoils of a top-grossing Fortune 500 company, the Sullivans are known as one of the wealthiest and most powerful families in the Northeast. One could never gather that from witnessing the firstborn Sullivan's meager lifestyle. Tucked away in the corner of the Catskill Mountains, the Sullivans called New Paltz their home, a small town with as much history as it has charm. And if the residents of New Paltz knew of Alex Sullivan's beginnings, they never let on.

According to Natasha Sullivan, Alex's mother, Alex had a dream, an American dream. He gave up his heritage to make it on his own, building a successful gym from the ground up and training the locals as well as professional boxers and athletes. His most widely known client was Nick "The Strangler" Stacks, a young man from humble beginnings, who is well on his way to becoming the next UFC Heavyweight Champion.

Alex's widow, Morgan Sullivan, is no stranger to tragedy. Her own twin sister died at the young age of seventeen in a prom night car accident. After the death of her husband, Mrs. Sullivan withdrew from the public eye while the story of her husband's tragedy exploded over social media. Even three years later, on the anniversary of Alex Sullivan's tragic death, *#foreveryoung* and all articles associated with the popular topic continue to make headlines.

Unbeknownst to Ms. Sullivan, the mayor of New Paltz, Grant Peterson, enacted a paparazzi ban within the town limits, a strategy that is completely unheard of in current times. It seems Mr. Peterson claimed that his taxpayers deserved privacy and respect, regardless of who they were. Against the wishes of Sullivan Enterprises, all reporters and photographers were run out of town.

While the elder Sullivans were searching for answers as to whom their son married and her plans for his fortune, they were surprised to find out that Morgan Sullivan had no idea of her husband's riches and that she frequently worked hours of overtime to cover their expenses.

When Ms. Sullivan became a widow, she also became part owner of her late-husband's gym, Sullivan's Gym, alongside Alex's close friend and MMA fighter Nick Stacks. The first few years as new business owners were difficult for the pair, and Sullivan's Gym suffered, but by year three, Ms. Sullivan and Mr. Stacks figured out the particulars of running a business and turned the gym back into the successful company that it was when Alex Sullivan ran it.

After spending years as business partners and running partners, Mr. Stacks and Ms. Sullivan began a relationship that was suggestive of more than just being co-owners. Even a stranger's eye can see that they are entangled in a less-than-professional relationship. Just don't ask any of the residents of New Paltz about these two, unless you want to be personally ushered out of town by the mayor himself.

On an ending note, according to the Sullivan's board of trustees, the estate left to Ms. Sullivan remains untouched.

Doug Richards, contributing reporter.

Next to the article is the picture of me and Nick kissing that night the buck attacked him.

I fold the paper up with shaky fingers and find it funny that Michelle didn't mention the buck that tormented them the entire time they were living as my neighbors. Nor did she mention that she and Doug pretended to be married and moved in next door to me to get information. Half of this I had no clue of—the apparent fact that Alex's family planted them there, that they wanted to know about me. I bet they planted that piece of plastic in my phone line to listen in on my conversations. All they had to do was ask. Instead, they were like every other person who *liked* and *shared* Alex's story—they wanted to talk about it, but they never bothered to talk to the one person directly involved. Me.

I fold the paper up and shove it into my bag. When I look up, Nick is watching me from across the parking lot. I can dwell on the fact that they deceived me, or I can just let it go. I decide to let it go, and I walk toward Nick's open arms and welcome the tight hug that he wraps me in. When I look up, I notice that Nick's eyes squish and crinkle in the corners as he smiles down at me. He looks at me like my mother looked at Tori and Alex.

"What were you reading?" he asks.

"Nothing important."

Being here in Nick's arms is all that I need. Here, I am the wanted one. I am the expected one. Believing in each other and fighting for each other healed our brokenness. We fought and we won.

ABOUT THE AUTHOR

M. R. Pritchard is a lifelong inhabitant of upstate NY. When she is not writing she is a NICU Nurse, wife, mother, gardener, aquarist, book hoarder and science geek. She holds degrees in Biochemistry and Nursing.

⭐ Connect with me ⭐

ⓐ amazon.com/author/mrpritchard

Ⓦ http://mrpritchard.com/

Ⓑ secretlifeofatownie.blogspot.com

ⓕ facebook.com/MRPritchard

Ⓟ pinterest.com/mp30/boards/

Ⓨ @M_R_Pritchard

Acknowledgements

Thanks so much to all of my readers, fans, and people who nominated this book on Kindle Scout!

To Caroline and Paul and the rest of the Kindle Press team, thank you so much for navigating me through this journey and for your hard work and enthusiasm for this project.

Many thanks to my husband, who has supported me every step of the way on this crazy journey, and who keeps my wine fridge, beer, and hard liquor stocked. I love you, Jorden.

There is no way I would have ever found the courage to complete this book, and continue on with more, if it weren't for my encouraging family, friends, and fans. I thank you all from the center of my heart.

To my beta-readers, Heather, Jessica, Nora, Cynthia, Teari, and Melissa: You girls rock!

There are not enough thanks I could give to Kristy Ellsworth. Thank you so much for all of your hard work and dedication to this project and all the others.

Author Note:

Thank you for reading! I hope you enjoyed this novel! Since there is no better way to share the love of a book than by word of mouth, please take the time to leave a review on Amazon.com or Goodreads.com or tell a friend about this book.

M. R. PRITCHARD

Other Books by M. R. Pritchard

<u>Science Fiction/post-apocalyptic:</u>
The Phoenix Project Series:
The Phoenix Project
The Reformation
Revelation
Inception
Origins

The Safest City on Earth
The Man Who Fell to Earth
Heartbeat

Asteroid Riders Series
Moon Lord
Collector of Space Junk and Rebellious Dreams

<u>Steampunk:</u>
Tick of a Clockwork Heart

<u>Dark Fantasy:</u>
Sparrow Man Series

<u>Fantasy/Fairy Tale Romance:</u>
Muse
Forgotten Princess Duology
Midsummer Night's Dream: A Game of
Thrones